ALSO BY JAMES LASDUN

*Delirium Eclipse and Other Stories*
*A Jump Start (poems)*

# THREE
# EVENINGS

# THREE EVENINGS

STORIES

James Lasdun

FARRAR STRAUS GIROUX

NEW YORK

Copyright © 1992 by James Lasdun
All rights reserved
Printed in the United States of America
Published simultaneously in Canada by HarperCollinsCanadaLtd
First published in 1992 by
Martin Secker & Warburg Ltd, London
First American edition, 1992

Library of Congress Cataloging-in-Publication Data
Lasdun, James.
Three Evenings: stories / James Lasdun.
p.    cm.
I. Title.
PR6062.A735M5    1992    823'.914—dc20    91-36468    CIP

In various shapes and forms, these stories have appeared
in Grand Street, Encounter, Paris Review, Twenty Under
Thirty-Five, Best Short Stories 1987, Fiction magazine,
New Writing. 'Trumpet Voluntary' was published by
The Guardian, which commissioned it for their series 'UK 2001'.

*For Pia*

# Contents

# Ate/Menos,
# or The Miracle

1

Sunday morning. I awoke to a murmur of faint anxieties. The day held nothing and nobody in store for me. I rose and prepared my breakfast. The radio was tuned to a religious programme, but I hadn't the resolve to switch channels.

How was I to fill the big blank freedom of the day?

I thought perhaps a walk, and set off along the high street, intending to continue in a straight line until I had had enough, when I would board a bus and return home.

Little traffic, few pedestrians, mute sounds and colours. A lamp in the distance had failed to extinguish itself with the dawn. The silver light hung blurred in the white sky like a dissolving pearl, and by its mild incongruousness drew my attention to the ordinariness, the celestial ordinariness, that Sunday morning confers on London streets.

How immutable the bricks and paving stones and plate-glass windows looked. Tarmac and hoardings, railings, pillar boxes, drain-lids . . . Sometimes I would give anything to glimpse a chink in the monumental armour of stasis with which the material world cloaks its fabled Heraclitean flux. I looked hard at the sturdy frontage of a bank, as if staring would make its weighty masonry shimmer and melt. How weak I felt, how powerless.

I mention these details in the hope that they might shed some light on the series of events that followed; a series that began with my entering a church, where a service was in progress, and committing a sacrilege.

## 2

As I reached the ugly portals of St Simeon's, I found myself slowing to a halt. I could hear strains of a hymn, the voices of what must have been a pitiful congregation swamped by the swell of the organ. I am not a believer, let alone a Christian, and had seldom been near a church since leaving school. Nevertheless, as I stood there listening, I experienced a strong, commanding urge to go inside.

*Ate* and *Menos* are the words Homer uses for states of mental intoxication induced in humans by gods or other supernatural agencies. *Ate* drives a man to commit demonic acts of rashness for which he is duly punished. *Menos*, which comes frequently in response to a battlefield prayer, is moral spunk, a sudden access of energy, confidence, strength.

What it was that possessed me is best described in these archaic terms, there being no adequate modern equivalent; though whether my actions were performed under the aegis of *Ate* or of *Menos*, I am to this day unsure.

I pushed open the heavy wooden door. An usher—blue-rinsed and clad in thick tweed—stepped smiling from a pew and handed me a small blue pamphlet with the words *Holy Communion* printed on it.

There were twenty or so worshippers. Vicar, organist, and the three-person choir were all dressed in clean white surplices. The place smelt of cold stone and candlewax. A few faces craned round to look at me as I entered an empty pew; old, placid faces that paused a second to register this unlikely addition to their numbers. The priest was reading from the pamphlet. I flicked through it and found my place.

It can hardly be termed an act of rash folly to enter an Anglican church on a Sunday morning, but nevertheless I knelt down on my threadbare hassock with the same sensation of wild recklessness I might have felt had I been installing myself in a brothel or an opium den.

I was struck immediately by the familiarity of the words the priest was saying. For a moment I thought I was experiencing a memory rush from boarding-school days of compulsory chapel. But the familiarity carried no poignant reverberations of that anguished period, and I realised the echo was of a note played much more recently. Played only this morning in fact, when I had been too listless to switch channels on the radio. At the time, I had not been conscious of hearing a syllable of the service it had been broadcasting. But now, as I listened to the priest's measured, impersonal voice, the words set their identical precursors, implanted that morning in my unconscious, chiming resonantly in sympathetic harmony, like so many ringing glasses, and the whole utterance hummed inside me with a vibrant power.

'Take, eat, this is my body . . .'

Slowly, on limbs for the most part decidedly unsteady, the members of the congregation filed from their pews, to form a queue in the aisle. The organist played long, reedy, wavering notes as one by one these shaky old souls dropped to their knees to receive their bread and wine. And when my blue-rinsed usher stepped forward to take up the rear, pausing at my pew to look at me questioningly, I began to understand why I had come here.

A feeling of abandon took possession of me as I moved towards the priest. I had never done this before and was not entitled to do it. The priest moved and muttered in a sphere of candlelight and such daylight as the stained glass admitted from the sunless sky. He had the composed air of a man entirely taken over by his role. The operation of his limbs as he carried gleaming chalice and paten from head to head was conducted with deft, balletic economy. There were now three people ahead of me. I kept my eyes on the fluted drapery of the priest's brilliant white robe. Two people. Tremulous organ notes filled the air. One person . . . and there I was, kneeling before the linen-draped altar, unchallenged, accepted by the priest without a second's hesitation or glance of appraisal. *The body of Christ* . . . I took the wafer, thin and translucent like an honesty pod, and held it melting on my tongue. *The blood of Christ* . . . metallic tang, iron-rich, finally sweet . . . I rose; I had known exactly what to do. The stray waverings of the organ collected themselves into a soft melodic tune that sounded like the music of forgiveness. Somewhere among the tumult of sensations welling up inside me I heard the peace of God which passeth all understanding being commended to me. Daylight flooded in through the opening door. As I left the church, the priest took my hand warmly in both of his.

'I do hope we shall see you here again.'

I smiled, and stumbled past him onto the high street.

3

The same high street; an altogether different pair of eyes observing it. What had I done? Nothing at all, I told myself. Nothing of any consequence. Why, then, did I feel this preternatural energy tingling in my body? I was fuelled, burning.

I had stolen fire from Olympus, by which I mean that I, a non-believer, had tapped the energies of ritual without submitting myself to the acts of faith it asked in return. I wasn't sure whether I felt demonically mischievous or consummately benevolent: that woman approaching me twenty yards off—I had it in me to run forward and throw her under a bus; but equally, had she in that moment chosen to throw herself under the same hypothetical bus, I could, in the split second available, have flown forward to pluck her from the wheels before they crushed her.

I must have been staring hard at this particular woman while I entertained these thoughts, because as she came nearer I realized she was looking at me in an inquisitive way—an expression on her face of guarded interest that burgeoned gradually into a nervous smile of recognition.

'You're Matthew Delacorta,' she said, coming to a halt two or three paces in front of me. 'We met in Edinburgh.'

I stopped and looked at her closely. She was carrying a bag full of groceries, fingers in black net gloves peeping up from beneath it. Her blouse, skirt, and hat were all black too, but trimmed with velvet and astrakhan, so that they seemed fashionable rather than funereal. A spray of crimson flowers was pinned to her lapel. She looked ten years older than me, a face in the process of exchanging hue and bloom for form and character; more than enough allure in it to make me feel glad to have been stopped in the street by its owner. But it was her voice more than anything that I noticed in that first moment: high and pure, modulated like the voice of an exquisitely brought-up girl of seventeen—full of fervent wonderment and respect, at once timid and confident, startling in the way that early recordings of legendary sopranos or film stars can be, through the hints they give of a distant, dreamier age. Hearing this voice weave its way through the syllables of Matthew Delacorta, I wished instantly that this *was* my name, and that this woman and myself had indeed met in Edinburgh, a city I have never visited in my life. I was about to tell her she was mistaken, when she spoke again:

'You mayn't remember who I am . . . I'm a friend of Felix, you know, who did the lighting for you. He introduced us after the show. My name's Madeleine . . .'

Lucky Matthew Delacorta, that his imperfect acquaintance

with this woman should have left her so eager to claim acknowledgement from him. There was an urgency in her voice, behind its diffidence—a determination to be recognised. She gazed at me, at Matthew Delacorta, with her eyes wide open, a look almost of pleading on her face. I paused before answering—I wanted to linger in this flattering delusion of hers for as long as possible.

And in that pause it dawned on me, as the reader will have guessed, that I had it in my power to extend this delusion artificially.

It was with a sense of breaking through into an opulent, forbidden, and altogether unfamiliar realm of living that I smiled slowly at this stranger and said, in as relaxed and charming a voice as I could muster:

'Madeleine. Of course. I thought I recognised you.'

She rewarded me with a look of pure elation, and made no effort to move on. Clearly more was expected of Matthew Delacorta, and I had no intention of letting him down.

'How are things?' I ventured.

'Oh . . .' She shrugged her shoulders, nearly causing a bottle of Cointreau to tumble out of her plastic bag; then, with a rather graceful clumsiness, patting it back down with her chin. '. . . Things are all right . . . not perfect . . . I was supposed to be doing Iphigenia in May, but the money . . .' She finished the sentence with an eloquent tilt of her head.

'Oh dear,' I said, 'what a shame'; then added boldly 'You'd make a terrific Iphigenia.' *Terrific* is not a word I use, but it came to my lips of its own volition and sounded startlingly appropriate. She quickened visibly with pleasure at the compliment.

'Oh, do you really think I would?'

'I do,' I said, then rashly, for the sake of colour, added that Aeschylus must have had her in mind when he wrote the part.

'Euripides.' A brief look of doubt shadowed her face, but I

think it had less to do with my mistake than with my hazarded guess at Delacorta's style of charm. The camp hyperbole hadn't quite rung true with her, although there was evidently no serious damage done because, as she dismissed the doubt (she had probably been scarcely conscious of it anyway), she tried immediately to assuage any embarrassment the error might have caused me, with a bluster of platitudes about how impossible it must be for someone as busy as me to remember anything at all.

'I suppose,' she went on, 'things still are frightfully busy?'

'Well, you know . . .' Although I had begun to form a plausible picture of our respective circumstances, I was far from ready to risk anything detailed. 'There are various projects on the go' was all I was prepared to offer.

'Gosh . . . I'd love to hear about them . . .' She looked down at her groceries. 'The thing is, Kiku's at home and I ought to get back . . .' She bit her lip and studied me a moment. Bumping into Matthew Delacorta was obviously quite an event for her, and I could feel she was loath to let him go. I wasn't greatly surprised, therefore, when she invited me—nervously, her eyes alight with timid hope—to come home with her for a cup of coffee.

'I'm only round the corner.'

I made a show of consulting my watch. I was conscious of the double power of my position—my own power over the spirit of Delacorta and Delacorta's evident power over Madeleine. The knowledge burned in me like a draught of something hot and invigorating. Involved in it was a complicated sense of danger, which I felt largely on Madeleine's account. How alarmed she would be if my mask slipped and she realised she had brought home an impostor. Should this occur, it would be like finding ourselves on a high wire, and while I would feel safe in the knowledge that I intended her no harm, she herself could know nothing of the kind.

'That sounds very agreeable,' I said, 'if you're quite sure.'

'Oh yes . . . I mean, if you have the time . . .'

We set off, back in the direction of St Simeon's Church. I was wondering who or what Kiku was, and trying to compose an innocently probing question, when Madeleine said, 'What you told me about Kiku was so true. I don't suppose you remember a word of it, but I've never forgotten . . .'

I smiled and gave a non-committal shrug.

'You said there were infinite solutions to the problems of happiness, and Kiku's was almost certainly among the more successful.'

Well, there was nothing to be gleaned from that, other than a mildly ominous whiff of Matthew Delacorta's personality.

'Oh yes,' I said, 'I remember,' and tried to laugh it off as a piece of nonsense.

'No.' She sounded serious now. 'You meant it, and it's been a great source of strength to me.'

I was going to have to play Kiku by ear. Meanwhile, there was Felix, my lighting man—

'So how's Felix these days?'

'He went off to Sydney . . . didn't he tell you?'

'No, he never did actually . . .'

'Probably too shy . . . they were all shy of you. It must be very strange for someone so young to have that effect . . .' She tried to give me the indulgent smile of a seasoned woman, figuratively patting a brilliant young man on the head, but the smile was strafed with such visible anxiety, such genuine awe, that it quickly retreated, leaving behind the faintest of blushes.

'Terrific guy, Felix.' I sensed that, as Delacorta, I could heed or ignore her remarks as I chose; that she would willingly follow in whatever direction I took the conversation.

'Hm . . .' She looked into the opaque sky, and out of her gaze flowed silence as eloquent as speech. I saw dimly—as if blurred in the silvery clouds she was staring at—the tangled line of a life coordinated by love and sorrow.

'Here we are,' she said finally. A shimmer of excitement passed through me as we stepped into the spacious, gloomy hall.

4

The dark, musty atmosphere of a house furnished with heir-looms; treasured possessions, inherited without the cash to maintain them; dust-covered trunks in the hall . . . We climbed to a living-room crowded with oils in chipped and tarnished gilt frames. A battered grand stood in a corner, baring a row of carious, yellowing keys. Its top was laden with silverware —candelabra, vessels, a miniature silver phaeton—all badly in need of a polish. Great curtains of dark green velvet, pep-pered with moth-holes and mildew spots, were drawn across the windows. Madeleine switched on a lamp, the shade of which was patinated with dust, so that only a hint of illumi-nation was able to escape. She sat down on an ancient sofa with intricately carved wooden pillars supporting its back-rest, dust-coloured stuffing hanging from the wounds in its uphol-stery. Beside it was a coffee table bearing a wooden bowl filled with limes and tangerines. These shone with a jewel-like gleam, improbably mineral, as if it were they that had drained all the splendour from the room and were thus alone respon-sible for its faded, threadbare appearance.

'I'll make some coffee,' Madeleine said.

I sat quite still without thinking while she was gone. I was riding high on my *Ate*, my *Menos*—whichever it was—and although I was aware of the extraordinary precariousness of my position, the awareness was far too remote to cause me any anxiety. My being here was meaningless, in that it was founded on a deception. And yet it felt, in a mysterious way, purposeful; as if deception were only what the first, most superficial analysis laid bare, whereas in the last, something altogether different was waiting to be uncovered.

The silence in the room was broken by a muffled thumping sound. I sat up and looked around, trying to locate its source. It seemed to be coming from the room next door, a slow beat pounding through the wall. I was about to investigate, when Madeleine reappeared.

'That's Kiku,' she said, putting two glasses down on the coffee table. 'I thought we'd have cocktails instead of coffee. But come and meet Kiku first.' The thumping grew louder and faster.

Kiku's room was locked, the key still in the door. Damp, human-smelling heat reared up at us as Madeleine opened the door. I stepped inside, onto an amazingly soft orange carpet strewn with toys. A girl of seven or so, in pigtails and a flowery frock, was standing on one side of the room, hitting the wall with her head. The wall was padded, covered in quilted gold corduroy to a height of about eight feet. The few pieces of furniture in the room were similarly padded.

'Kiku sweetie, stop it. Kiku. *Suky.*'

The girl turned to us with a smile. 'Kiku,' she piped.

She was Madeleine in immaculate miniature: her mother's big dark eyes and delicate bones, her mother's high, dulcet voice, the same atmosphere of faint misalignment about her, but the sweetest, the most engagingly attentive of smiles.

'Kiku, then. Say hello to Matthew Delacorta. She won't, though.'

The girl ran halfway across the room, stopping suddenly to kneel on the carpet and pick up a toy aeroplane. The wings of the plane seemed to wilt in her hand. They drooped down like petals on a dead flower. I realized then that it was made of felt, and that all the other toys in the room—the dolls, the building blocks, the menagerie of furry animals jumbled around the bed in the corner—were made of similar materials. The room was entirely devoid of hard surfaces.

Kiku waved the plane around, jerkily following its movements with her head, still smiling. Then, with a sudden, vicious twist of her arm, she hurled it tail-first at the wall, which it struck soundlessly.

'Suky's her real name, then?'

'Yes, remember I—'

'—Yes of course . . . Hello, Kiku . . .'

I walked towards the girl kneeling on the floor. I had an impulse to hold my hand out in front of me as if I were approaching a timid animal that might want to sniff a bit of me first. She was still smiling, bunching up the freckles on her cheeks and nose. She looked as though she was on the point of coming out with one of those comically candid remarks that children make—*Will you give me some sweets*, or *I don't like you*—but she said nothing at all. I knelt down before her, conscious of the close attention of her mother standing in the doorway. Delacorta was being assessed for his rapport with the child.

'Hello there, how are you, then?' I patted her head. Her smile was beginning to look like a fixture, a sort of benign facial disfigurement.

'I'm Matthew,' I said.

She was looking straight into my eyes, her own still dew-bright with infancy. 'Matthew,' I repeated. I took her little hand and gave it a squeeze. It lay unresponsive in my grasp.

'She's very lovely,' I said to Madeleine, still holding the limp hand.

'She's everything to me.'

'I can see why.' I turned back to the girl. 'Aren't you a sweetie, Kiku?' Silence. 'She's a shy one, isn't she?' At this Madeleine gave me a peculiar look, as if I'd said something wildly inappropriate. 'I mean, ah . . .' I stopped myself from blustering, 'shy's the wrong word, I suppose . . .' Madeleine looked a fraction more hopeful. And then quite suddenly the whole situation—the thumping, the padded walls, the soft

toys, the rigid smile—snapped into place, and I recognised
the child's condition. I assumed an expression of pious concern. 'She *is* happy, though, isn't she, one can tell . . .'
Madeleine's eyes were glistening. As I rose to my feet I noticed
a dark patch spreading on Kiku's flowery frock. She was still
smiling, no longer at me, but at the space my head had just
vacated. Madeleine led her out of the room after me. 'Naughty
Suky,' she said. 'Kiku,' the girl replied. 'Join you in a moment,'
Madeleine said, steering me back into the drawing-room with
a touch of her still gloved hand. Somewhere in the depths of
the house I heard a lavatory flush.

5

'I call this one Piña Madeleina. Tell me what you think.'
Madeleine handed me my fourth cocktail. Like all the others
it was foul, and in a distant way that foulness was reflected in
the intimacy that the alcohol had established between us: a
bogus intimacy in which I attempted to be wittily rude, while
she pretended to be delightedly shocked.

I took a sip and held up the glass before me.

'Too sweet, too thick, toothache,' I declared.

'Oh, Matthew! You monster!'

Kiku was in the room with us, lolling on the floor, flitting
from chair to chair, banging her head against things until her
mother got up from beside me on the sofa to stop her . . .
She provided a point of choral return for the conversational
lulls, as a cat or a baby does. But it made me uncomfortable
having her there—being faced with the disconcerting problem
of having to square her perfect physical presence with her
complete mental absence. I found it difficult to believe that
she was not pretending; that she would not suddenly shimmer

and melt into laughter and tell us how silly we were, how stupid it was of us not to realise.

'Tell me a story, Mr Delacorta,' Madeleine said. 'Felix said you were a great story-teller. He said you could hold the Company spellbound.' She took off her net gloves at last and, with the overemphatic precision of someone pretending to be sober, laid them hand to hand on the coffee-table. Her naked fingers were streaked red. I stared at them, startled, for some moments, until I realized she must have put on the gloves before her nail varnish had dried.

'Go on,' she said, ignoring the sight, 'spellbind me.' She snuggled back into the sofa.

I stared up into the shadowland between the curtain pelmet and the ceiling. Not being an imaginative man, I could no more create a fictional human being *ex nihilo* than I could a real one. But I sensed trailing behind Madeleine's request— far behind it and nebulous as the fleeciest end of a vapour trail—the unmistakable scent of sexual promise. At that distance it did not greatly excite me, but the possibility that it might if I were to get closer was enough to make me rack my brains for a scrap of an anecdote to reconstruct for her.

I might have been silent for ten seconds, or ten minutes; drink had brought us into harmony with the secret elasticity of time. The darkness at the ceiling seemed to swell out and engulf me. I was adrift when the idea came, let loose in space. I spoke, and the sound of my voice was like a faraway disturbance. The story I told required no imagination; it was the truth, no more, no less. But as I told it, I felt the kind of nacreous, distempered thrill that accompanies the telling of an ingenious lie upon which momentous decisions will hang.

'Sunday morning,' I heard myself say, 'I awoke to a murmur of faint anxieties. The day held nothing and nobody in store for me. I rose and prepared my breakfast . . .'

I told her of my indecisiveness in the face of the big blank freedom of the day, of my walk and the odd compulsion under which I had entered the church of St Simeon. *Ate* and *Menos* had not yet occurred to me as the alternative analogies for my behaviour. I kept to the facts; the sacrilegious communion, the preternatural energy tingling in my body as I left the church—

'I was fuelled, burning. I had stolen fire from Olympus . . .'

'What do you mean?' Madeleine asked, reaching with her streaked hand towards Kiku, who was revolving the fruit-bowl with a finger and had started to spin it out of control.

'I mean that I, a non-believer, had tapped the energies of ritual without submitting myself to the acts of faith it asked in return . . .'

I told her of the woman walking towards me, the purely hypothetical way in which she had first entered my consciousness, her looming into actuality as she accosted me with the name of Matthew Delacorta.

At this point Madeleine's face lit up with the realisation that she was the woman and I myself the man. She was hooked. The words that left my lips as fact reached her as fiction. I had no hesitation in revealing to her that I was not Matthew Delacorta. She listened with a drugged smile that seemed to struggle towards some more specific expression when I disclosed (or, as she would have received it, *invented*) the subterfuge by which I had inveigled my way into her home.

'A shimmer of excitement passed through me as we stepped into the spacious, gloomy hall . . .'

She looked around the living-room as I described it, relieved to be able to fall into her familiar attitude of delighted outrage as I itemised the mildew spots, the dust, the sofa's wounded upholstery. I spared her nothing of my reaction to Kiku. She heard it with a glazed look of entrancement such as I have sometimes imagined is found on the faces of the dead when their guardian angel shows them the life they have lived, with all the parts that were once obscure to them rendered luminously visible.

It occurs to me that between reality and my account of it there was precisely the difference that lies between the two mutually exclusive boxes contained in a drawing of a transparent cube. The lines were identical, but her cube was the inversion of my own. What happened in the process of this inversion was not so much a sacrifice of truth as a diminishing of it to an entirely valueless quality. And under this devaluation, the currency of everything else became arbitrary. I was neither Matthew Delacorta nor myself, but a trick card on which either would show, depending on how it was held to the light. The ramifications of my connection with Madeleine—was she succumbing to my charm, to Delacorta's, to my version of his charm—went on like an infinite mathematical series. We had entered a realm where we were subject more to the laws of physics than to those of human nature. And just as, under random stimulus, a quark is said to leave its own equivalent of a spoor along all the paths that it might have taken but did not, as well as along the one it did, so I felt myself refracted into a mirror-hall of multiplicit possible selves, each one of them pressing a ghostly claim to being the sole channel through which these events were flowing. It was a vertiginous feeling.

'Tell me a story, Mr Delacorta . . .' I concluded, with a smile.

'What a *peculiar* story,' Madeleine said wonderingly, and gave a long, melodic sigh. The clear sound was like the sight of the gleaming limes and tangerines whirling beneath Kiku's fingers—a seam of pure tone lacing the shabby, crepuscular atmosphere of the room. Something in the contrast made the blood tingle in my capillaries. I downed the last drops of my cocktail and asked for another.

'Make it bloody this time. A Delacorta Haemorrhage.'

17

Madeleine giggled, and walked unsteadily out of the room. Alone with Kiku, I performed some magic. I produced coins from thin air and exhibited them in the palm of my hand. I slid a cigarette into my ear and extracted it from my mouth. I balanced a chair on my foot and set it spinning. My life's accomplishments; and Kiku gazed through them with her attentive smile, taking in nothing.

'Suky,' I said.

'Kiku,' she corrected me.

'Suky,' I repeated.

'Kiku.' There was, I thought, a note of anxiety in her voice.

'Suky.'

'Kiku.' Her eyes widened with alarm at this challenge to the single piece of herself she had chosen to share with the world. She looked agitated, and began to whimper. I felt I was on the brink of establishing contact with her, that all it required was the correct incantation in order to focus her mental processes onto me.

'Oliver,' I said, pointing at myself.

'Liar,' she replied without moving her lips, only of course it was not her but Madeleine, returning with the drinks, her voice barely distinguishable from the little girl's.

'Why are you lying to my daughter?' She tried to look proprietorial, drawing herself up and placing a hand on the girl's head, but found she had sufficient self-command only to initiate the attitude, not to sustain it. She sank down onto the sofa beside me, looking momentarily lost. I took the drink from her hand while she gathered herself. Then I took the hand too, and answered her question with a question of my own.

'Why are you covered in nail varnish?'

'Oh'—she looked forlornly at her hands—'I keep doing that . . .'

I drew her close to me and murmured something intimate,

sentimental, and untrue. Sweet odour of boudoir; roses and strawberries . . . I kissed the proffered lips. There was more pink powder on her skin than I had thought, and an almost invisible pale down glimmering over it. She looked at me warily, assessing the balance of pain and pleasure to be had from a man ten years younger than herself. She tilted back her chin, showing me three cross-hatched furrows circling her neck: this is how I am, the half-conscious gesture said; stop now if you think you might hurt me later on. I drained the cocktail in one gulp and followed her out of the room as the last of the sweet emulsion crawled down my throat.

6

The inner sanctum . . . Kiku thumped in her padded cell, while Madeleine and Matthew Delacorta made love in the pot-pourri of crumpled sheets, lipstick-stained tissues, and jumbled clothing strewn about Madeleine's bedroom.

I was there as an intimate observer, having loaned Matthew Delacorta the use of my body for the occasion.

'Oh, Matthew,' Madeleine said, 'Matthew Delacorta.'

I smiled for him. The sugar-fizz of pleasure swarmed at my groin. But just as it is neither the glass nor the mercury that registers heat in a thermometer, but the eye that looks at the two in relation to one another, so my body, temporarily removed from my ownership, remained in an entirely mineral relation to this pleasure, even to the moment of climax.

In the dozy period that followed, I became aware of two things. First, that Kiku was no longer thumping in her cell, and second, that my *Ate*, my *Menos*, had abandoned me.

It lay on the floor, a gloppy pearl tied up in the rubber sheath that Madeleine had produced from a little snakeskin treasure chest.

As I grew conscious of myself there in the bedroom of a stranger, I had a glimpse of the scale of my deception. It was so colossal I could hardly credit it.

'I can feel your heart thumping,' Madeleine said drowsily. 'What's bitten you?'

'Nothing.' I swallowed the short word before it was finished. My voice—I could feel more than hear this—had lost all trace of its preposterously confident timbre, and vibrated now to the higher, breathier pitch of fear. The room looked dismal; debris that had suggested dry, scented rose petals took on the bleak look of mere refuse. Madeleine's eyes were closed. I tried to still my beating heart. I was afraid she would open her eyes and see not Matthew Delacorta but me. My fear was vicarious as well as on my own account: I myself was as much the object of it as was the more practical danger I felt, of being found out. And this in turn, ironically but with a perfectly consistent logic, began to make me feel close to Madeleine in a more innocent way than I had previously. I wanted to communicate a tender, protective concern for her well-being. I wanted to reassure her that she was safe from her intruder while I was around. I pulled her close. She responded sleepily to my kisses. The alcohol on our breath had not yet gone rank, and there was a muzzy, intoxicating atmosphere around us.

'So you like me,' she murmured contentedly.

For the first time, a feeling of raw, carnal desire for her took hold of me.

'Very much,' I said.

We went at each other with deep, probing kisses. Out of shyness, or caution, or plain modesty, she had put on a short night garment when we had first gone into the bedroom. I had tried to slide it off her, imagining that I was expected to, but she had signalled resistance and I had left it alone. Now, however, as my hand slipped between it and her skin, she raised her pelvis and let me pull the silky fabric off her, so that for a moment her naked body was thrust fully towards me, a scarlet flush spreading from her neck to her nipples, breasts dilated wide and shallow under their own gravity, looser flesh bunched spongily at her stomach . . . Outside, the first rumblings of the returning weekend traffic had begun, and the light was paling. The room, filtered once more through desire, resumed its aura of rosy *déshabillage*. Overcome again by modesty, or whatever it was, Madeleine pulled me tightly against her, wearing me. She drew up her legs and took me inside her.

'Shouldn't I put a thing on?' I whispered.

'No . . . it's safe.'

As Delacorta, I had been granted a limited intimacy—held back from ultimate communion by the thin veil of a prophylactic. As myself, however, I was given the full, ravishing candour of her nakedness enclosing my own. O Rose, thou art sick! The invisible worm . . . did I destroy her in that moment? Was I with Satan or with the angels?

7

When at last we descended, it was not to the drawing-room but to the kitchen in the basement below.

A bearded man in an old corduroy jacket was sitting at the table, with Kiku on his knee. Madeleine did not seem in the least surprised to see him, although a visibly charged look passed between them. Before him was a plate of biscuits and a jug of overdiluted orange squash. On the wall behind was a gleaming xylophone of Sabatier knives.

'This is my husband,' Madeleine said, gesturing brusquely towards him, 'and this,' she held my arm gently, 'is Matthew Delacorta.'

My first thought was that, far from having deceived Madeleine, it was she who had all along been deceiving me, drawing me into a domestic plot which, if obscure in its details, was instantly familiar in its atmosphere of banal squalor.

However, the husband betrayed no sign of anger or jealousy. He merely looked me briefly up and down and said, 'He isn't Matthew Delacorta.'

I remember gaping at him, speechless. His words had the impersonal, dispassionate ring of a judicial verdict. I turned to Madeleine, assuming my hour had come. But it seemed I had underestimated her powers of self-delusion. She closed her eyes wearily. 'Oh don't be like that, Benedict,' she said, adding for my benefit, 'Husbands can be awfully trying.'

'He isn't Matthew Delacorta,' the husband repeated. His puffy, watery eyes (somewhere in them the melancholic stoicism of a drinker resigned to his condition) scanned me again. Kiku's rag-doll legs dangled from his lap. She stared at me.

Madeleine turned her back on them and lit the gas beneath a tarnished kettle.

'Take no notice of him, Matthew. He'll be off soon, won't you, Benedict? It's his turn for Kiku.' I sensed a quarrel between them of an antiquity that had turned it into habit. There was no pride left, even in appearances. I forced myself to recite the words the occasion demanded:

'Perhaps you know another Matthew Delacorta . . . ?'

For a while he didn't answer, but merely spread a hand out and looked at it gloomily, as if scrutinizing the state of his nicotine-yellowed fingernails. The kettle began to make knocking sounds. I was at the depressed heart of a family and wished I was elsewhere. I had a strong desire to cleanse myself.

Finally, without looking up, the husband said, 'I know Matthew Delacorta, and you're not him.'

Madeleine shook her head at me from behind him. A white rim had appeared around her tightly shut lips. Her eyes strayed over the Sabatiers, faltered, then returned to me with a wistful smile.

Her misplaced faith no longer amused or flattered me; I felt wretched. But for her sake I tried to make a stand. As politely as I could, I told the husband he had made a mistake, that I was indeed Delacorta, that I directed plays, had met Madeleine at the Edinburgh Festival through Felix, and was now as it happened looking for a Cleopatra.

'I'm hoping Madeleine will agree to audition.'

Madeleine stepped round and gave her husband a triumphant smile. He ignored her and said to me, 'What are you?'

Kiku twisted back her head and began to wriggle. A rushing sound came from the kettle.

'Oh go away Benedict. You wreck everything,' Madeleine said quietly.

'I can prove he isn't Delacorta. There's a picture of Matthew in Rosemary's book on the Fringe. It'll be in one of my trunks in the hall.'

He deposited Kiku on the floor and stepped past me without a glance. He smelt of rain and tobacco, a distillation of autumn. Madeleine breathed in slowly, to calm herself, it seemed. 'I'm sorry about this,' she said. She began to spoon tea into an enamel pot. Dried leaves scattered across a Formica surface.

'Perhaps I should go,' I said. 'I'll contact you about this Cleopatra audition.'

She looked at me, glimmering with hope, and with despair. She dropped the spoon and ran out of the room. 'Benedict,' she cried, 'Benedict, please . . .'

Alone with Kiku, I realised I had to disappear. Wisps of steam rose from the spout of the roaring kettle. I picked up a biscuit and held it out to Kiku. 'Here you are, Suky.'

'Kiku,' she said, snatching it from my hand. I poured her a glass of orange juice. 'Drink it, Suky.' Her eyes widened. 'Kiku,' she said shrilly. Steam poured from the kettle, billowing into the room, blanching the blades of the Sabatiers. As I held the glass to her lips, I felt a last convulsion of my *Ate*, my

*Menos*. From upstairs came the sound of remonstration. 'Suky,' I said, 'that's who you are, *Suky*.' She opened her mouth to whimper, dribbling out the orange juice. 'Suky,' I repeated, 'Suky.' The whimper grew louder. 'Kiku,' she cried. 'Suky.'

Her voice rose to a scream. Her face turned scarlet. Footsteps tumbled down the stairs. Her mouth began to shape the cry into strange, nonsensical syllables, as if she was groping for words—*gaa, bey, cooo* . . . I stepped, adulterer fashion, behind the door as mother and father burst back into the steam-filled kitchen. I vanished deftly behind their backs, taking the stairs three at a time, bounding across the hall without pausing to look at the book lying open on one of the trunks, while a high, grief-stricken female voice I could not identify cried, 'No', drawing out the word into an anguished wail that pierced the air as I ran from the house, repeating itself over and over: 'No, no, no . . . o . . . o . . . o . . .'

# Snow

M y great-uncle Dominic, the inventor, took me into the
small workshop that stood between the back of his house
and the large kitchen garden behind it. 'This will amuse you,'
he said, pointing to a box-shaped contraption with what looked
like a headlamp encased in it. 'It's called a stroboscope. They
are going to become very popular.' He switched on an electric
drill and brought it into the flashing, acetylene-blue light of
the contraption. With his free hand he adjusted the frequency
of the flashing, and I watched, enchanted, as the drill-bit
appeared to slow gradually down to a complete halt. 'There,
you see,' he said, 'it renders the most violent things harmless.
Touch the drill, go on . . .'

Such was his solicitude, however, that before I had raised
my small hand a fraction, he clutched it with his own. 'Now
let this serve as a lesson to you. Watch . . .' He brought a
piece of wood from the work-bench to the motionless drill-
bit. A harsh rasping came as the one contacted the other, a
flashlit spray of sawdust plumed out in a staggered curve, and
in a trice the innocent piece of metal had bitten clean through
the inch-thick piece of wood. 'There you are. If something
looks peaceful then leave it alone or else you get crucified.
The stroboscope makes machines look still because it only

illuminates one point in their cycle. Terrible accidents happen in factories where they have flickering neon lights . . . Now I must go and have a nap before Inge and I go out.'

Uncle Dominic was a man of extraordinary mildness. Family legend has it that his only retort to the irresponsible nurse in whose charge his son drowned forty-five years ago was 'If this sort of thing happens again you'll have to go.' He made his fortune when the patent for a guidance device he had invented was purchased by an aeronautical company, which then adapted it for use in naval missiles. After the war he calculated that he had been instrumental in the deaths of some twenty thousand people. The fact haunted him. He wrote countless letters to the press warning scientists to guard their discoveries from the military, and was much ridiculed for them. In an oddly inverted piece of *folie de grandeur*, he papered his workshop with the dead and wounded of Hiroshima, as if he had been personally responsible for the carnage. The projects he worked on became increasingly trifling as his concern over their possible abuse grew more obsessive. That winter he had perfected a machine for feeding minced chicken, at twelve-hourly intervals, to Salome, his beloved Persian Blue, so that he and his second wife, Inge, could take short holidays without troubling the neighbours to look after the animal.

He had also built the prototype of a hair-plaiting device for Inge, and as we returned from the cold workshop to the warm house, we heard Inge shouting from the bedroom upstairs, 'Come and get this wretched machine out of my hair. It's stuck—' Uncle Dominic quickened his pace, then checked himself. 'I mustn't run,' he said to me, 'you go and help her.'

Inge, twenty-six years my great-uncle's junior, sat at her dressing-table in a blue silk peignoir embroidered with tiny bright hummingbirds, the plaiting device sticking incongruously from her long golden hair. 'Ah. Little Thomas,' she said, 'how sweet you are . . .' I stood behind her disentangling the golden strands from the silver tines of the device as gently as I could. 'None of his machines work these days,' she whispered, as Uncle Dominic's footsteps approached the door.

He fell instantly asleep on the bed, while Inge had me brush her hair with her soft, ivory-handled hairbrush, and plait it with my own hands. I can remember wanting to tell her how lovely I thought she was, but having the courage only to let my all-licensed hands linger in that gleaming floss some moments longer than was necessary. She coiled the braid into a bun and fixed it with two tourmaline pins. 'Now go,' she said, 'while I dress,' and kissed me on my forehead.

I saw them off from the front entrance: my great-uncle immaculate in evening dress, the black of his tall gaunt frame and the silver hair repeated in his tipped ebony stick; Inge's sable stole collecting the first white crystals of the frozen evening. 'We won't be long,' she called to me from the bottom of the marble steps. 'Anne-Marie will look after you. If Mr Morpurgo arrives before we do, then . . . offer him a drink.' She climbed into the car giggling at the thought, and they drove off to their cocktail party.

I sat on the living-room sofa drawing Christmas cards for them, while Anne-Marie—or Claire or Gabrielle—buffed silver knives and piled them on a salver, where they gleamed like fish spilt from a net.

Mr Morpurgo, their dinner guest, did arrive before Dominic and Inge. He wore, as I remember, a yellow suit with pieces of brown suede clasping the shoulders and elbows. His face was a porous, piecemeal assemblage of unrelated features that could never agree on one expression. Smiles dissolved into scowls, then into parodies of misery, swiftly, and with no apparent reason. He was the kind of man who awakens in children their first sensations of snobbery. I offered him a drink, and when he asked jovially if I was joining him, I declined with a delicious sense of disdain. He addressed me as 'little man', but I knew he had only been invited out of pity, because his wife had left him, and it was Christmas Eve, and he happened to live across the garden. He tried to flirt with the au pair, but she feigned ignorance of English. He put on a French accent, as if that would help, and she quickly found an excuse to leave the room. He wandered about picking up and examining ornaments from shelves, and when I intimated that the silver-and-glass-framed wedding portrait of Dominic and Inge he'd pulled from its hook was fragile and perhaps rather special to them, he made a great show of replacing it exactly as he'd found it, smirking at me while he did so. 'Whatever the little man says,' he added and, in an attempt to amuse, clicked his heels together and saluted me.

The slam of the front door brought in Dominic and Inge, rosy-cheeked and vibrant from their cocktail party. As they greeted Mr Morpurgo, apologising for their lateness, I watched the powdery snow on Inge's stole melting into tiny seed-pearls that clung, sparkling, to the wet tips of fur. The arrow-heads of her pale blue high-heels were rimmed with moisture, and I remember this pleasing me, because it meant the snow was settling.

At dinner, Mr Morpurgo tried to draw out my great-uncle Dominic on the subject of his pacifism. 'Go on, admit it,' he kept saying, with what was presumably intended to be a roguish grin, 'you're deluding yourself. No real progress has ever been made in the name of peace or love. Greed, aggression, and lust—that's what motivates people. We're beasts really—I'm one, I don't deny it. I organise my life and work accordingly. Stab your neighbour before he stabs you, that's the only way. Admit it, go on . . .' Out of courtesy, Uncle Dominic made a token defence of his position, the lazy, tail-swishing defence a horse makes against a mildly irritating fly, and it seemed entirely proper to me that he should not waste energy doing battle with so unworthy an adversary.

After dinner he dozed on the living-room sofa, Salome dozing on his lap, while Inge and Mr Morpurgo played back-gammon, quietly accusing one another of cheating, and giggling quietly so as not to wake Uncle Dominic. Mr Morpurgo risked a stab at his sleeping host—'That's how he preserves his illusions, is it—by sleeping most of his life, and only waking up for the good bits?' Inge smiled sadly at her husband and said nothing.

As ever, no effort was made to send me to bed, although Mr Morpurgo twice expressed his amazement at 'the little man's stamina'. I went, eventually, in the wake of Uncle Dominic, who, roused by the bite of Salome's claws, declared himself a little sleepy, and retired, wishing us all a happy Christmas. When Inge came up to say good night, she let me unpin her hair, unfurl it, and separate the three golden locks which she rustled back into one dishevelled tress before returning to Mr Morpurgo.

I found myself very suddenly wide awake long before the dawn of Christmas Day. I postponed opening my stocking until my great-uncle and aunt would have woken and I could open it on their bed, the quilt wrapped about my shoulders, while they received my tribute of delight in return for their generosity. Through my bedroom window the dark blue sky with its sprinkling of stars coaxed pale shades of silver from the snow-covered garden and surrounding houses. The snow on the garden was pristine, except for a dotted line that ran across the centre from our house to the one opposite, like the perforations between two stamps seen from their white, shiny backs.

I put on my slippers, went downstairs to investigate, and yes, parallel with two sets of snowed-over footprints leading out from the back door, past my great-uncle's workshop, was a set cut freshly into the crisp snow, the arrow-heads pointing back into our house.

The significance of these footprints remained in chrysalis

within me until the recent death of my great-uncle reminded me of the occasion; though by then I, like everyone else except perhaps Uncle Dominic, knew all about Inge's affair. The sight thus provided me with no sorrowful descent into knowledge. It did, however, give rise to a tableau which now seems a peculiarly expressive coda to my great-uncle Dominic's life.

The busy Christmas morning rituals on the day itself demanded I put the image of the footprints temporarily out of mind. At lunch, though, it rose once more from its suppression. The ten or twelve assembled relatives had finished eating, and we were leaning back in our chairs telling stories and sipping *eiswein*. Whether it was an excess of that extraordinary distillation of frost-corrupted grapes, or the air's intoxicating fragrance of tangerine peel, burnt brandy, and cigar smoke, or the way the candle flames were splintered and multiplied in the table's debris of silver cutlery and dishes, I don't know; but something released in me the image of those tracks again, catalysing a thought that seemed to me astoundingly clever and well worth the immediate attention of the company.

'Uncle Dominic,' I called out in my shrill voice. The table hushed, and my great-uncle's eyelids opened a crack. 'Your stroboscope is like snow. There were footprints leading to the back door this morning when I got up, and I've just thought . . .' but to my chagrin the relatives at once resumed their conversations in unnecessarily loud voices. I piped louder, but my ingenious explanation—that all the action happens *between* the footprints, so that only the moments of stillness are made visible by the snow—was drowned by my relatives' voices that rose with mine, fell briefly at intervals when they thought I'd given up, then rose in chorus again as I persisted, so that all Uncle Dominic was allowed to hear were the disjointed words that rang out during the brief pauses.

He looked perplexed for a moment, but made no attempt to hear more than the babble permitted, and soon let his eyelids drop again. I was finally silenced by Inge's mother, who asked me, with a fatuous (though unreturned) grin at her daughter, whether I thought those footprints might have been Father Christmas's. Mortified by this snub, I fell into a sulk from which I did not recover until I had flown back to my parents, who worked in a place where Christmas is not celebrated and where snow has never been seen.

# The Coat

It was a light summer coat of yellow velvet with a silk lining. The velvet was soft and smooth. It might have been cut from the petals of an enormous primrose.

It had been given to Muriel by a dear friend (this was the term she had settled on), a veterinary surgeon, who had treated Muffy, Muriel's dog, for the numerous ailments she was suffering from when Muriel had first taken her in.

The pockets with their deep silk interiors were very cool to the touch. There were three buttons: ivory-coloured, with sunflowers moulded in relief on each. The shoulders were styled a little outward, a little upward, not padded but giving just a hint of regal breadth. The skirting tapered inward —a note of playful severity —stopping just high enough to disclose its owner's ankles, which, as the dear friend constantly averred, and as Muriel did not mind admitting herself, were something a seventeen-year-old girl could have been proud of.

In fact the whole garment flattered her. The colour revived a lustre in the remaining honey colour of her hair; the cut did credit to her figure, which if nothing else was still erect. Wearing it Muriel felt a little more radiant, a little lighter-hearted than usual. It was, she sometimes felt, like being sheathed in an emanation from her own youth.

For this reason she wore it sparingly. She was in good health, not yet sixty, still worked in the college where she had been registrar since her husband's death. But after all, one's youth was not something to be called up indefinitely; its residue was volatile, like an ancient chrism that too much exposure might vaporise.

Then too, by an instinct for the higher subtleties of sympathetic magic, she made a point of never putting on the coat with a view to *inducing* livelier spirits; never wearing it to 'cheer herself up', as some of her more simple-minded acquaintances imagined they could by dressing up in some gaudy retrieval from the depths of their closets. No. She wore it only when the rare mood, the distant intimation of gaiety, was already stirring inside her. Then and only then would she wear it: not to coax but to facilitate, to enhance.

After checking the sky and the hall barometer (the dear friend had cautioned that water might spot the material), she would lift the coat from its padded hanger, swim her hands into the stream-cool sleeves, button up the three sunflower buttons, and step out from her small brick house (she preferred not to think of it as a bungalow), onto the lane that led to the village, pausing to smell a neighbour's honeysuckle, or buy stamps, or pick up groceries at the village store. Invariably someone would admire the coat, remark how well it suited her, how elegant she looked in it, how young, and she would answer graciously, feeling a sensation of calm delight arising in her, as if a cool flame were waving through her body.

The dear friend was a gentle, quiet soul called Donald Costane. Their attachment was more consolatory than passionate—they had come late into one another's lives—though once or twice a remote craving had passed through Muriel as she watched Donald's long, white, well-manicured hands pick their way through the mangy tufts of Muffy's ochre hair in search of sores and parasites, then lave themselves in disinfectant soap and rub each other dry with a crisply starched hand-towel. However, his regard for her appeared to be restricted to the scope of formal veneration. He admired her spirit, which he considered both proud and refined. He cherished a notion that the two of them were each other's reward for maintaining dignity in the face of unspecified suffering. It was understood that if they were not 'above' other people, they were at least 'apart' from them, in possessing virtues too subtle and discreet for the world to recognise; that they must bear their obscurity with fortitude, but that now at least they had each other to help them. Such, at any rate, was how she interpreted his attentions.

And in a very little time she came to see that the limits he tacitly set were not only sensible but were also conducive to unexpectedly rich and gratifying feelings; feelings that had more to do with possibility than actuality, suggestion than statement, with consummations subtly deferred that at another time might have been eagerly sought. So that their friendship had acquired the air of an eternal courtship: two parallel lines moving together over horizon after horizon towards some infinitely distant but perpetually beckoning point of convergence.

'I must admit I always believed I would come into my own at sixty,' Donald said once during a mild post-prandial haze. 'Even, would you believe it, when I was quite a young child.'

Muriel had laughed. 'It is a shame we didn't meet when we were younger,' she had ventured, then, realising from his abstracted look that she had missed the point, added, 'But perhaps we would not have recognised each other.'

He was handsome in his own way: shiny grey hair always neatly brushed and set; dignified profile; grave, pouchy eyes that seemed to indicate a bottomless fund of sympathy. He collected Victorian pewter, dressed in well-cut suits or sports jackets, drove a plushly upholstered car, and was dependably punctilious in the matter of flowers and notes and little gifts at appropriate moments—all of them well-chosen, though none as bold, as presumptuous, as the coat, which he had presented Muriel with after their first outing to London, when she had complained of looking and feeling like all the other dowdy provincial ladies at the theatre.

It had astonished her, arriving by delivery van one afternoon, in a shallow box the length of a body, wrapped in several layers of tissue; lying there buttoned up, primrose yellow, with a fresh rose in its lapel, and a little mauve envelope with a note saying simply *For the Metropolis*.

He spoke little about his past and seldom asked Muriel about hers. The agreement seemed to be to banish all ghosts for the duration of their meetings; to create passages of perfect happiness while they were in each other's company.

Their outings were elaborate, and no doubt costly, though Muriel herself never saw a bill. They occurred perhaps once every six weeks, more in summer, a little less in winter. They had quickly established themselves as the high point in Muriel's routine, becoming downright necessary after her son, Billy, joined the navy and was out of the country for most of the year; so that, aside from the trivial solace of gossiping with the neighbours, there was effectively nothing but Donald between herself and whatever it was that pressed upon one during the quiet afternoons when there were no letters to write, no cardigan about to go at the sleeves, nothing to weed or prune in the garden, and one could see as if through glass straight into the empty ocean of the day.

But the coat.

There had been the occasion of the Losing of the Button.

It had happened during one of the outings to London. Donald had picked Muriel up as usual at eleven o'clock in the morning. They had driven to the city, eaten lunch at an Italian restaurant in Charlotte Street, strolled to the embankment, and taken a boat ride along the river. Gulls, bridges, boat crews

flat in the water like pond-skimmers, the Parliament buildings
rising from the thumbed bronze Thames like needles of car-
amel combed up out of molten sugar . . . Donald had enquired
in his solicitous way after Billy; Muriel began a lament about
her son's deficiencies as a correspondent, then, hearing the
unpermitted note of complaint in her voice, stopped herself
and changed the subject, which Donald graciously pretended
not to notice. After a drink at a newly restored Victorian pub
in Shoreditch that Donald had wanted to investigate, they had
gone to a musical in the West End, finishing off their evening
with a light supper at a crowded brasserie in St Martin's Lane.

It had been an entirely satisfactory outing. Donald had told
amusing stories about some of his animal patients, for whom
he bore a tender and unashamedly personal affection. The
musical had been cheerful and tasteful. The weather had been
sunny but cool, and she had worn the coat all day except when
they were indoors.

On the drive home, as she was drawing it a little tighter
against the evening chill, her fingers had registered a bobble
of thread where the middle of the three sunflower buttons
should have been.

She waited until Donald stopped for petrol on the motorway,
when she took the opportunity to make a search of the car; to
no avail. Suspecting Donald would feel obliged to turn back
in search of the button if he thought she was upset, and equally
that he would be offended if she affected not to care, she
refrained from saying anything when he returned to the car.

But all the small contentments of the day, stored up in her
mind to be fondly relived later, had seemed to pour out of her
in a single rush of annoyance.

The following morning she phoned the coat's makers and
found that neither the coat nor the buttons were being man-
ufactured anymore. Without pausing—she did not want to
give herself time to question what she was doing—she drove

41

herself to the station (driving in the city made her nervous) and took a train to London. Thinking she had probably lost the button towards the end of the outing—else she would surely have noticed it—she began retracing her itinerary of the previous day in reverse.

Nothing had been found at the car park or the brasserie. The cloakroom attendant at the theatre in Piccadilly had a box with odds and ends in it that people had left behind in the theatre: keys, gloves, fountain pens, a pocket-sized television, but no buttons of any description. Staving off her disappointment, Muriel took a bus to Shoreditch and walked to the Victorian pub. With its gilded cherubs and mirrors, its scrim-shawed narwhal horns and enormous buttoned-leather sofas, the pub might have been expressly designed as a haystack for the concealment of her particular needle. A group of young men, catching on to her predicament, made a raucous display of searching every nook and cranny of the lounge and saloon and public bar, much to the irritation of the other patrons. The exercise was as fruitless as it was embarrassing. And what with the commotion, the heat, and the smell of beer and spirits, it left her feeling distinctly weak on her knees.

She took a taxi to the little shack on the embankment that served as the offices of the pleasure-boat company. The lady who sold tickets remembered her; remembered the coat at any rate, as soon as Muriel described it, and seemed as concerned as Muriel herself at the loss of the button, entering Muriel's by-now-unconcealable anxiety with a fullness of sympathy that made her feel at least that she was not being wholly ridiculous. It did not, however, produce the button.

At the Italian restaurant in Charlotte Street, the bow-tied manager who had attended to her with studied gallantry the day before, helping her both into and out of the coat, today not only failed to remember her but treated her with thinly veiled suspicion, only grudgingly allowing her to inspect the cloakroom at the back of the restaurant, eyeing her all the while as if she had come here to steal the silver. Glimpsing herself in a mirror on the way out she had had an inkling why. She looked frayed, haggard, dishevelled, and a little crazed.

So she had emerged into the afternoon heat of the city.

There was an hour before her train left, and she wandered slowly towards Charing Cross. A muffled sensation came into her. She felt dimmed somehow, and cut off from the buildings and people passing on either side of her. Confronted with the failure of her mission, she began to wonder why she had embarked on it in the first place. What had possessed her to waste a day in such a senseless fashion? If she couldn't replace the button, she could find three others that would look just as nice as the sunflowers. Really, she told herself, it had been altogether rather a shameful exercise. And futile.

But even as she admitted these things, something in her rose obstinately to her own defence. There *was* something worth clinging to in the idea of perfection. A thing once blemished was never the same, however much you forgave it. At any rate, she herself was so constituted as to be sensitive to the small things that made the difference. If that was a fault in her, then so be it. She was not responsible for the aspirations of her own soul.

She marched on, squinting into a glare that seemed to radiate equally from the street, the sky, and her own exhaustion. Turning a corner, she came to a crossroads where the flow of people and cars was held up by what appeared to be the demolition of an underground public convenience. Giant excavating machines were grouped around a crater in which were exposed—among clay, rubble, creeper-like armatures of plumbing, and some patches of broken mosaic—several door-less toilet cubicles with the white porcelain bowls still nakedly in place. Verdigris-streaked pipes led up from them like stalks from enormous onion bulbs. A horrible odour hung in the heat. She tried to hurry by, but the cordoned walkway past the site had narrowed pedestrian traffic to single file. For several unpleasant seconds she was caught in a slow-moving human crush. By the end of it, a sweat had broken out on her lip and she was feeling dizzy. Just as she emerged, a pigeon flew down slantwise right across her face, so close she felt a buffeting of hot air on her eyelids. She gave a soft cry and put her hand to her heart, which had at once begun knocking in her chest. The pigeon landed in one of those arid patches of earth left unpaved at the base of city trees. It scrabbled there with its wormy toes; a filthy bird, looking as if some passing god of the metropolis had seen fit to breathe life into a broken lump of pavement with a smear of oil on it. Muriel caught its bulbous eye as she paused for breath. Cigarette butts, sweets wrappers, and bleached excrement lay around it on the sandy earth. It hopped between two gnarled claws of root, jabbed at the ground, and then took off with a wheezy flapping.

And there between the roots, pristine and gleaming, as if the pigeon had just that moment laid it, was the sunflower button.

A sensation of hot triumph had come into Muriel as she stooped for it. She felt both elated and defiant, as if in retrieving the button she had confounded some opposing law of existence.

It was warm from the summer heat, and mysteriously communicative as only an inanimate object can be.

She had been even more sparing in her use of the coat after that, restricting herself for the most part to admiring it in passing as she picked something less hazardous from her bedroom closet. She hung it on its padded hanger, with a net bag full of cedar chips to keep away the moths. It was hanging there, of course, the weekend her son, Billy, came to visit with Vanessa.

## The Coat

An only child, born late in a marriage already entrammelled in mutual if seldom articulated grievances, Billy had seemed from an early age pale and indefinite, as if stretched thin by the diverging motions of his parents. As a boy he had been timid; as a teenager, after his father's death, he had seemed to make a point of forming friendships with the shiftiest-looking, most unappetising specimens of local youth. What they got up to when they sloped off together on Friday and Saturday evenings, Muriel had preferred not to imagine, though from an instinctive appraisal of their collective character, she had suspected it was confined to the pettier forms of disorder, and she silently thanked her stars that her son had not been cast in a more vigorous mould. Later, after he had left school, he had seemed to settle down contentedly, or at least without conspicuous dissatisfaction, to a job at a nearby estate agent. Gratified by the apparent change, Muriel began to enjoy his company; even to allow herself to depend on it. And while it was true that occasionally when she spoke to him he would meet her look with a expression of rather childish bewilderment in his eyes, Muriel had not suspected him of seriously chafing at the outward circumstances of his life. It had come as quite a surprise then, when he had arrived home from his job one day, a few months after the Falklands War, and announced that he was going to join the Royal Navy.

He had met the girl, Vanessa, on his first weekend of shore leave after a long tour of duty in the Arctic. It was unlike him to bring home a girl, particularly one he had known for no more than a few weeks. Sensing something momentous, Muriel had gone out of her way to extend a welcome. But her overtures towards Vanessa—a pallid girl with a loose, large mouth and long fingers varnished pink at the nails—were received with what appeared to be a mixture of suspicion and amusement, and it had soon become apparent that the weekend was going to be a trial.

By Saturday night the young lady had distinguished herself by lounging around the house with next to nothing on, feeding Muffy chocolates till the poor thing was sick, sitting on Billy's lap at mealtimes, spoonfeeding him, cooing baby talk at him, signalling at him while Muriel attempted to make conversation with him about his tour of duty, until with a sheepish grin he had sidled off after the girl and followed her upstairs. Muriel had not been born yesterday, but there are certain sounds that she considered a mother's ears better off not hearing, and she had had to go outside and prune the roses in the twilight rather than endure them, though even there she had heard her son's name called out in a startlingly piercing cry: *Billy, Billy . . . My God.*

It was as she had suspected. On Sunday morning Billy took her aside to ask what she thought of Vanessa. She had begun to make a reply, choosing her words carefully, with an equal view to truth and tact, when Billy interrupted to tell her that he had proposed to the girl and that they were going to get married on his next leave.

So that Muriel had felt it her uncomfortable duty to take them to the Sandbourne Hotel at lunchtime, for a celebratory glass of champagne . . . The girl's idea of dressing up had been to exchange her negligee for a lederhosen outfit with a loose, sleeveless top that seemed designed to draw every male eye deep into the ripe shadows of its shoulder halters. It had certainly caused a stir in the lounge of the Sandbourne, and the girl had clearly revelled in the attention, letting her eye stray about the room, babbling her silly nonsense in a loud voice that got louder the more she drank.

Under the circumstances it was difficult not to contemplate the crude perils awaiting Billy in his long absences at sea. But with luck perhaps the young lady would find herself unable to manage even the few months of solitude that lay ahead of her, and Billy might learn his lesson without the added humiliation of being actually married to his teacher.

# The Coat

Shortly before they left the hotel, something behind Muriel caught the girl's attention. Her eyes kept moving slyly to a point just over Muriel's shoulder, then sliding back to Billy's with a look of suppressed mirth. A few times Billy looked covertly over at the bar, then met Vanessa's glance with expressions that changed gradually from perplexity to the same reined-in hilarity, as if he was slowly cottoning on to some private game. Muriel did her best to ignore it, but at last turned round to see what they were looking at. There was an elderly man in a brass-buttoned blazer sitting at the bar: red-faced, white-haired, and with long, stiff, white moustaches twirled and waxed at the ends and sticking out absolutely horizontally above his lip. He was drinking gin and tonic and sitting with a very straight back. He looked with a stony or perhaps merely blank expression at Muriel's party.

Muriel turned reproachfully back to Billy, but before she could speak, Vanessa broke out with a peal of giggles and, after a feeble attempt at self-restraint, gave in to a fit of wild and rather terrifying laughter, which seemed to Muriel, however mysterious its precise cause, to be formed unmistakably of an inseparable cruelty and dirty-mindedness, and which twisted and crumpled the girl until, with tears streaming down her face, she had run off to the ladies' room.

That afternoon Muriel had decided it would be in everyone's interest if she absented herself from the house for a few hours. Apart from anything else, it might earn her a little of Billy's attention in the evening.

On the pretext of errands to run she drove off with Muffy to the nearby reservoir, where a footpath led around the shore.

People were out sailing in dinghies—snub-nosed Mirrors, and the flotilla of pretty, leaf-shaped Larks owned by the Sailing Club. It had been warm for days, and dry for most of the summer. The water level had sunk quite low, leaving a wide band of dried froth and ribbon weed on the pebbly shore.

Muriel clipped the lead to Muffy's collar and set off along the dusty footpath, bordered by the reservoir on one side and on the other by a flat wilderness of broom, gorse, and bilberry bushes. There was a smell of warm creosote from the Water Authority huts dotted along the shore, and an occasional dank algal breath from the lapping water carried upward on the breeze.

The place had always had a calming effect on Muriel, and it was not long before she began to feel a little less agitated.

She thought about Billy and Vanessa, and reflected that a father might have been useful to Billy at this moment in his life; even his own father, who had maintained high standards in his judgments of others, if not of himself. It was a pity, too, that Donald and Billy didn't get on—not that anything had been said, but it would be hard to imagine Donald offering to take the boy aside for a chat, let alone Billy submitting to such an offer.

Anyway, much as she loved her son, she knew that he was in some respects a fool, and that even if he was saved from this particular folly he would sooner or later find another one to commit in its place.

And then too, she thought with sudden gentleness, there was always the chance that Vanessa herself would improve. She was very young, after all. The shrillness and flimsiness of her outward manner might disappear over time and reveal a decent sort of soul. Her faults might not be deep; at any rate might not be irredeemable. You never knew what might happen to a person; it was a mistake to trust only in the worst.

A couple with a Labrador approached along the footpath. Muffy stood still to be sniffed, then sniffed the Labrador in return. She trotted towards the owners with her tail wagging, and Muriel let her stay a moment to be patted, though she kept the leash tight and watched her closely: Donald had said Muffy had probably been beaten as a puppy and would never be a hundred percent dependable.

She had appeared at Muriel's door one winter morning, her skin covered with bald patches and sores, and her skeleton visible beneath it. One ear had been badly chewed up, and one hind leg was in the air, apparently too tender to put on the ground.

Muriel had thrown her some bacon rinds, which the dog came warily forward to snatch up, limping off with them through the wet grass into the woods at the end of Muriel's back lawn. That evening she had returned, soaked and shivering. Muriel had thrown her some more scraps. The dog gobbled them, this time staying where she was and staring up at Muriel with her head cocked to one side when she had finished. Muriel had been touched by the sight and had called her inside, giving her more food and putting down a blanket for her on the floor of the cloakroom.

An acquaintance had recently suggested she get a dog for the companionship now that Billy was gone. She had taken no notice of the idea, never having considered herself a dog lover, but she found it difficult to turn the animal out of the house the next morning, and she soon realised she was becoming attached to the creature.

It had sharp, almost dainty features, like a very small Alsatian. Its cindery ochre coat had a reddish tinge on top that suggested red setter. After a few days Muriel had decided to adopt her and inquired about a vet to have her examined. It was in this way that she had met Donald.

Under his care, the dog recovered from her sores and grew back the fur on her bald patches. After a few weeks in a splint, the fractured bone in her hind leg mended perfectly. She lost her slightly unpleasant derelict odour and began to smell of ginger biscuits, if rather stale ones. She grew healthy and sleek and alert, turning in fact into a very pretty animal, with bright girlish eyes and a way of tilting her head to form a certain pathetic expression that never failed to arouse a pang of protective affection in Muriel.

Her nervousness had been slower to cure. She barked furiously at anyone who came to the house, and had once chased the child of a neighbour out onto the road, after which Muriel kept her tied up whenever she was outside. But in time the sedate rhythms of Muriel's life seemed to soothe the animal, and she had grown less noisy and excitable, becoming even a little bit slothful in recent months.

Muriel passed the Sailing Club, which marked the halfway point of her circuit. The sun was low in the sky, and a lance of light had begun to probe across the reservoir. From the far shore ripples shot across the water like footprints of a swift, invisible herald. A breeze blew up. Sails filled out and surged forward, tilting over as they were hauled in for speed.

Muriel remembered bringing Billy to the Sailing Club once when he was a small boy, and watching anxiously as the little Lark he was put in with an instructor raced off across the water at what had seemed a dangerously unstable angle. He hadn't enjoyed the experience any more than she had, and never showed any desire to repeat it: a fact she had not failed to remind him of when he had told her of his intention to join the navy.

The breeze died, then came back, stiffer than before. By the time Muriel completed her circuit, the reservoir had blossomed with brightly striped spinnaker sails billowing out in front of their craft and towing them along so fast that even the smallest cut a wake of orange light on the water. For a moment she stood and watched. They were lovely to look at, and she felt gladdened and lightened by the sight.

She drove home in good spirits, exercised and refreshed, sanguine about the chances of a civilised final evening with her son.

There was a note on the kitchen table when she got in:
*Gone to the pub. See you later.*

Assuming this meant they would be back in time for supper, Muriel put the casserole she had prepared into the oven and set the table. For a while she sat in the living-room reading the papers. But she was unable to concentrate, and fearing that her good mood might not survive if she sat there with just her thoughts, she went back outside to finish pruning the roses.

It was almost dark by the time she finished. Billy and Vanessa had not returned. She raked up the pruned stalks and carried them in bundles to the steel basket incinerator at the bottom of the back lawn. Putting in as many as she could, she poured petrol over them and set them alight. Flames shot up into the dusk. A few pearl-sized drops of water glinted in the firelight, falling to earth. She hadn't realised it had started raining.

Back inside, she ate her supper and cleared it away. Thinking it would be a triumph of sorts if she were to wait up for Billy and Vanessa and receive them without a trace of reproach, she went back into the living-room and had another go at the papers.

But the silence of the room, so familiar to her, and usually not oppressive, made her suddenly desolate. It really was a little inconsiderate of them to disappear like this, she couldn't help thinking, though she immediately chided herself; probably Billy had wanted to celebrate with some of his old friends from the village. Well, that was understandable. She resisted the temptation to feel hurt by him; there was no limit to how far you could slide in that direction once you started.

She stood up and went upstairs, thinking her best bet would be to go to sleep.

To her surprise she could smell Vanessa's scent as she went into her bedroom. She turned on the light. The slide door to the closet was open. She went over to inspect it. A pair of high heels on the floor had been tipped over. A tweed jacket had been taken out and put back with its collar twisted. There was a padded hanger with a net bag of cedar chips at a gap where the row of clothes had been divided. The yellow coat was gone.

Muriel sat back on the foot of her bed, a little stunned. For a while she neither moved nor formed a thought, but merely sat, coiled into herself like a person who has just been hit. Then gradually she began to make an assessment of the situation.

Obviously the girl had not taken the coat in order to spite her. She knew nothing of its preciousness to Muriel. She had taken it because the evening had turned out to be cool and she needed something to wear. No doubt she had asked Billy permission, and Billy had told her to help herself.

It was unfortunate that the weather had broken, but Vanessa could hardly be blamed for that. Anyway, Donald's warning that rain would ruin the velvet might well have been alarmist—he did tend to be a little overcautious. But even if he was right, so what? It was only a coat, after all, and one shouldn't make a fetish of such things. She had perhaps set too much store by it in the first place; certainly her day in London in search of the button filled her with a half-shameful feeling whenever she remembered it.

These last reflections were formed more in a spirit of wishfulness than conviction, but they helped Muriel stave off the feelings of annoyance that had begun to rise in her.

She felt it necessary to do this; in recent months she had noticed herself becoming prone to fits of irritation, often for quite trivial reasons. Something would vex her, and before she knew it she would have passed into a dream-like state of silent fury, where the most violent punishments would be meted out in an atmosphere of obscure malediction. She would emerge from these states feeling shaken and vaguely guilty, as if after an overindulgence. She had no wish to end her days in a permanent twilight of bitterness and anger. Why such a fate should threaten her, she had no idea; these things were apparently not in one's hands. But it was becoming a matter of conscious vigilance to maintain a pleasant disposition and keep the more disagreeable tendencies of her imagination in check.

She no longer had any desire to go to sleep, and went back downstairs.

Passing the open door of the cloakroom she saw a short red suede coat on a hook and remembered that Vanessa had brought this with her. Because of the fine weather, she had not worn it all weekend, and Muriel had forgotten about it. Seeing it now was like being struck again. For this argued, did it not, an indifference verging on contempt?

A feeling that had in it both dismay and bewilderment came into Muriel. She pictured the girl putting on her own coat, then discarding it and running upstairs to Muriel's bedroom and rifling through her closet, trying on one thing after another, posing in the mirror, calling out to Billy for approval. The idea was peculiarly distressing; it unfolded in Muriel like an extremely unpleasant physical sensation.

So that it was again necessary to get a grip on herself.

She went into the living-room and sat in an armchair without turning on the light. She thought of ringing Donald—it might have helped to talk to someone—but dismissed the thought. Idle telephone chats were not a part of their arrangement. Donald would assume a calamity had occurred and start flapping, then wonder why she had rung. Worse, he might attempt to rise to the occasion and encourage her for once to pour out her heart, and she dreaded to think what that might bring forth. Either way, she was certain to regret disturbing him.

And at this she found herself struggling against a sudden impulse to denigrate, even to revile, her friendship with Donald. What sort of friendship was it, after all? What did it mean? An infinitely deferred promise of love; an offer of intimacy that would never survive being taken up . . . She thought of him with his sombre, considerate manner that seemed to invite confidences yet somehow always contrived to deflect them; his elaborate attempts to procure a frail feeling of enchantment that was really nothing but a kind of sweetened anaesthesia . . . Was that all she could hope for any longer? A feeling of disgust rose in her: for his tepid notion of happiness, for her own collaboration in it, for his fussy habits, his clean hands, his cabinets with their carefully labelled curios, his cautious driving, his conscientious gifts and notes . . . God, he was like the ghost that didn't know it was a ghost. He was like the void of a person not there . . . And if their time together was an improvement on their respective solitude, it was only as an exchange of the despair that knows it is in despair for the despair that imagines it is not, and is therefore even further from hope . . .

She felt as if the darkness of the room were seeping into her soul. Morbid and bitter thoughts began to take hold of her. She saw herself quarrelling with Billy and Donald—even heard herself spit out the withering remarks that would bring about these quarrels—then sitting alone here in the living-room like someone in a ship drifting towards some vast and empty darkness.

She stood up and went outside.

Cool, light rain was falling steadily now, pattering on the grass, swishing through the woods at the end of the garden.

She walked to the garden gate and stood looking along the lane that led to the village. In her mind's eye she saw Vanessa putting on the coat as she and Billy left the pub and going out into the rain. She followed the girl's carefree steps, imagining the first drops of rain falling onto the material of the coat. A sharp spasm of anger went through her, but it was followed by a feeling of helplessness.

Smells of wet soil and wet vegetation filled the air, sweet and fresh under the acrid driftings from the incinerator. In a few days the first brown marks would be appearing on the roses. Trees that had fallen in the big spring winds would start succumbing to mosses, fungus, lichen; the wood growing soft, pulpy, then powdery, eaten up by insects and mould, blackening, disintegrating, disappearing into the soil . . . She had heard woods described as being like an hourglass: the life sifting from the trees into the earth, then the hourglass turned around and the life sifting back into the trees. The new grew off the old, the living off the dying. But it was never the same thing that grew back. Life poured into you, then the hourglass was turned and it began to pour out of you.

The moon was high in the sky above her, muffled in cloud, its light falling in showers through the upper air, glittering in dimness on the wet hydrangeas and feathery yew shrubs of the house opposite, pooled in the giant leaves of the gunnera plants in the border along the fence, dripping from branches, pouring in plaited trickles from the gutter onto the garden shed.

After a while she heard the girl's voice from far off. The two figures appeared, Vanessa hanging on Billy's arm, both of them walking a little unsteadily. The girl's hair was plastered to her skull, giving her face a rudimentary look: a knot of sense organs. The coat looked more silver than yellow in its sheen of rain and moonlight.

# Trumpet
# Voluntary

M y fortunes had been in steady decline since the events of '97. After the closure—deservedly punitive, I hasten to add—of the college where my wife and I worked as administrators, I attempted to turn my lifelong hobby to good account, and did actually find work as a trumpeter on some of the recordings of patriotic music just then coming into vogue. However, it was not enough to keep us in any of the more secure neighbourhoods, and following the police act of '98, we were obliged to leave the city altogether. Our borough could afford only the lowest level of policing and went rapidly downhill. It was soon no place for a respectable couple to be bringing up a young daughter.

We moved west, to the village of Haughton Pusey, near Bristol. My wife's cousin worked in the Lord Lieutenant's new offices and had promised her a job as a typist. It was a humble position, but not without its advantages; by then the emergence of such figures as the Lord Lieutenant and the Lord High Sheriff from their century or more of ornamental obscurity was well under way. As a nation we were in the first throes of rediscovering the ceremonial heritage that is of course so much of our life today, and to be employed at the court of one of these personages—ours virtually ran the affairs of the county

—was not only immensely prestigious but also gained one the material gratitude of such of his supplicants as one was able to assist, whether it be a shopkeeper in search of a fresh meat or citrus charter or a transporter hoping to increase his monthly allowance of petrol. My word, we were popular in those days!

I was able to use the connection to secure myself a position as second trumpet in one of the county's licenced dance bands. As well as the patriotic music I have already mentioned, we had been seeing quite a revival of traditional swing and big-band music. One of the young princes had been championing it so enthusiastically that nobody of any discrimination would listen, let alone dance, to anything else. Our stipends as musicians were small, but at least steady, and there was seldom a week without an engagement at a dance hall, or a gala, or a house party for one of the better families of the county.

It was on one such occasion that, to my everlasting shame, I allowed myself to become involved in an act of monumental collective folly that brought this phase of our lives to an abrupt end. Over forty years have passed since that evening, and I am now an old man, but I can assure My Lady, if she should ever do me the honour of reading this, that I am still able to blush for my former self.

We had been playing at the Marquess of Avon's New Year's Eve party in Becclesley Hall. Midnight had passed. The year 2001 was in its second hour. Most of the guests had departed, and those that remained were somewhat the worse for wear. We, the band that is, were tired, and by now also a little tipsy—not that I offer this as an excuse. The intervals between numbers were growing longer; the numbers themselves slower and more sentimental. It was perhaps not surprising that those of us left in the ballroom should suddenly find ourselves plunged into one of those strange moods of desolate sadness that were so much a feature of postwar life. By that I refer of course to the second Falklands War of '97, where His Late

Majesty, after being obliged to authorise the military's ousting of Mr A.'s prevaricating government, had courageously ordered the destruction of Buenos Aires, winning us the war, at the cost—negligible compared with what we had gained—of international ostracism.

A desolate sadness, yes; and one that, mimicking perhaps the state of the country itself regarding the rest of the world, was poignantly isolating in its effects. One by one the gowned or bow-tie-and-tailed figures retreated into corners and shadowy alcoves to sit alone with the nameless, inconsolable anguish that had come upon them.

We had stopped playing for the moment. Sighs echoed in the lofty room, and there were even sounds of muffled sobs. Companionship was no comfort at these moments. Indeed, such was the extremity of the emotion that few people could even bear the sight of their own loved one while under its cloud. (Perhaps, incidentally, it will amuse the reader to learn that these spontaneous expressions of feeling were the origin of the glorious annual Ceremony of Good Air, in which we now give thanks for our present peace and prosperity.)

Into this maudlin atmosphere came a few whistled bars of a song that we were all familiar with. I think a guilty thrill passed instantly through every one of us. The song had been placed under a royal edict banning it from both public and private performance, but since the whistler turned out to be none other than our flamboyant, eccentric young host, the Marquess of Avon, nobody cared or dared to silence him. Moreover, the truth was that at that moment we were all susceptible to the piercing melancholy of the tune. Tears were streaming down His Lordship's florid face, and as he whistled he performed a sort of shuffling dance with a jeroboam of champagne. The tune was a mariachi air, a slow beguine that had been made famous by one of the charity-pop groups who were at that time so active in international affairs. The proceeds of the record—it had been an enormous hit—had gone to help the survivors of Buenos Aires, and although it had been banned in Britain from the start, there were few people in the country who had not at one time or another found themselves being stirred uneasily by its bittersweet words and cadences. After all, it had been the chant of our students throughout the summer of the anti-Windsorian rioting in '97. In those days it was called, simply, 'Buenos Aires'.

Well, to cut a long story short, it wasn't long before the Marquess had prevailed on us to strike up the song and thereby rouse and reunite his remaining guests into a last, slow, gliding dance of remembrance which, if not consoling, had at least the mildly intoxicating effect of an act performed in defiance of a prohibition.

I may say that, even at the time, my better judgment was urging me to remove myself from these disgraceful goings-on, but I am afraid that my baser instincts were one with those of the degenerate crowd surrounding me. A sweet sorrow ached in me, and as I raised the trumpet to my lips, I too succumbed to the blandishments of that haunting melody.

Still, like others no doubt, I imagined the affair would be dismissed as mere excess of party spirits, should the authorities ever get wind of it, especially since it had taken place in the home of one of our leading families. It came as quite a shock, therefore, to learn the following day that the Marquess had been arrested for treason. He was hanged a week later. The band lost its licence. Our instruments were confiscated. My wife was dismissed from the Lord Lieutenant's office. Our daughter lost her place at school.

In retrospect I realise we were treated with undeserved leniency by the authorities. At the time, however, all I could see was the ruin I had brought upon myself and my family. For a month or two we clung to the outer margins of respectability, living on our paltry savings and on the calling-in of a number of favours my wife had performed over the years. However, the stark fact of destitution loomed larger every day.

On our transportation convoy from London to Haughton Pusey we had glimpsed enough of life in the unpoliced wildernesses where the dross of society was left to its own wretched devices to know something of the horrors that awaited us. Even Jean, our daughter, seemed to sense the seriousness of our predicament. We found her one day on her way to post a pile of letters addressed to the parents of her old school friends. I still remember how pitifully she begged us not to open them; it turned out that the dear thing was trying to ease our burden by offering herself up for adoption!

My wife, understandably, could scarcely bring herself to speak to me during this period. Nevertheless she did not, as I did, succumb to the lethargy of despair, but instead threw herself into ever more frantic efforts to ward off catastrophe, and it is once again she whom I must thank for our deliverance.

Realising we had no hope of finding further employment in our own county, she had, with great difficulty, obtained job listings from places farther afield, an exercise I had thought futile since the expense of moving was simply more than we could bear. However—Providence be praised—just as we were reaching the very end of our scant resources, she found an advertisement (it was in the *Northumberland Gentleman's Gazette*) that fit our own description so well, so *snugly*, that without fancifulness I can compare it with the way the sculpted, blue-plushed interior of my trumpet case—my *ex*-trumpet case, that is—fitted round the intricate tubes and valves of the instrument it had been built for.

A couple was wanted, with a daughter aged eleven to thirteen. Couple to have compu-secretarial and administrative skills. Musical skills also appreciated. Daughter to be clean and well-mannered. Relocation expenses would be paid.

You may imagine with what nervous eagerness we applied for the position. My wife's cousin was persuaded to write a letter of recommendation on official notepaper (that, Jean, cost you the pearls we had been saving for your twenty-first). A note arrived summoning us to Northumberland for an interview. There was a minor crisis over the matter of getting the Lord Lieutenant's office to process our travel permits in time. Given our disgrace, we had every reason to expect all manner of petty hindrances to this formality. My wife decided on a personal visit to the Lord Lieutenant himself—a fellow well known for his weakness for the female sex—and returned triumphant, though grimly uncommunicative as to the substance of the interview itself. I can report that I had enough delicacy not to press her.

Our furniture paid for the coach tickets, with a little over for the incidental expenses of the journey. We set off in a spirit of desperate optimism, trying our hardest not to dwell on the consequences of an unsuccessful interview.

I am too much of a patriot to want to cloud this happy tale with ugly descriptions of our journey to the far north of England. Those were harsh times. Travel had very rapidly become a dangerous affair. Resting places for legitimate voyagers were under constant threat of attack from gangs of ruffians roaming the countryside, and needed to be protected. There were rumours of a vast convoy of armed vagabonds at large in the road system itself, so that even in motion one felt at risk. Where violence and anarchy abound, the law cannot afford to be as subtle or temperate as we might wish. Suffice it to say that there comes a point where it is obliged to inscribe its signature in the human body itself. I refer readers still curious for details of the edifying sights that presented themselves to us along certain stretches of the M1 motorway to descriptions of the Appian Way, in ancient Rome, after Crassus had put down the revolt of slaves under Spartacus.

We passed the time speculating on our prospective employers, the Gilliehursts. All we knew of them was that they lived on a large estate in one of the northern ruralities still under Royal Protection, that their estate carried with it the responsibility for the local militia's brass band, and that, presumably, they had a daughter Jean's age, in need of a companion. I say 'presumably', because they had made no actual mention of this daughter in their note. But we could think of no other reason why they should want to encumber themselves with another couple's child. It was touching to hear Jean wonder aloud whether her new friend was going to treat her as a sister or as a sort of maid. 'I'll love her just as much whichever,' she said, gazing with humble adoration into her imagined future. We saw every reason to encourage her in these sentiments.

At the rurality border we disembarked, and trudged through driving rain to the tourism bureau for passengers not on official business. There, with a hundred other weary souls, we waited in line for our turn at the processing booth, a humdrum detail I mention only for the sake of an amusing little vignette of social history that followed. In those days, before the glorious moment of Windsorian Nationalism had fully flowered, we were still living in the wake of a mania for what was then known as 'private enterprise' (how quaintly Dickensian the term sounds now). Other than those under Royal Commission, every institution from the police force to the British Museum had been sold to private investors, and it had come to be considered virtually immoral for any service to be performed without money changing hands. In the ruralities, where the banking system no longer operated at full strength, this had an alarmingly direct application, as we were to discover when at last our turn came at the processing booth.

Over the speaking grille was a timing clock, which had to be started before the clerk would begin interviewing us, and which could only *be* started by dropping a ten-pound coin into a slot in its top. Well, we paid up, but imagine our surprise when at the end of the fourth minute the clerk stopped talking abruptly, without even completing his sentence, and in order to get him to finish our business we had to drop in another —our very last—ten-pound coin!

Once inside the rurality itself, we soon found ourselves in glorious sunshine, with nothing but a little flotilla of ornamental cloudlets to interrupt the exquisite blue of the sky. After our bleak journey, the countryside looked breathtakingly beautiful. Neat fields of crops, clear lakes and streams, herds of red deer, flocks of woolly white sheep with cheerful-looking smocked shepherds bearing crooks, pretty little Duraflint farm cottages with smoking chimneys and smiling housewives feeding geese or hanging washing to dry, and waving at our coach as we passed. The only vehicles on the road or in the fields were coloured the gleamingly clean, dark khaki of the Ruralities Fleet, all bearing the royal crest in gold. Here and there climate-control towers shone in the sunshine (under His Late Majesty's orders, these had been constructed to resemble Chinese pagodas and were dazzlingly gilded). Nowadays we take these visions of pastoral splendour for granted; but this, our first glimpse of our kingdom's future, filled us with an almost mystic sense of privilege at belonging to a country of such indescribable loveliness.

Coming to a hillier region, we observed what looked like dozens of glass spheres, about eight feet in diameter, cascading down from the highest summits at a tremendous rate, bouncing off spurs of rock into enormous glittering arcs, smacking into each other and hurtling apart like billiard balls, careering down through treetops, sloping fields, and scree, and plunging at last down one or other of several spectacular waterfalls into the reservoir beside our road, where they floated together *en masse*, like so many Brobdingnagian soap bubbles, until each was ferried back up the mountain by its own helicopter.

To our amazement, each of these spheres contained a pair of human beings in a harness suspended—so our guide later explained—from a sort of gyroscopic inner sphere that kept its passengers upright for the whole terrifying descent. It was of course the sport we now know as globe-crashing, and it had just that very year become all the rage among the more adventurous children of the local gentry.

'Perhaps your new friend will take you on a ride in one of those,' I said to Jean. The darling seemed rather frightened by the idea—she was a timid child—'though of *course*,' she was careful to affirm, 'I should go with her if she wanted me to.'

At last we were dropped off at the Gilliehursts' estate. The mansion was—is—a magnificent affair: a classic early work in the Tudor-hacienda style evolved in His Late Majesty's Department of Architectural Correction; all thatched gables and pantiled courtyards, black-and-white timber fronts and mosque-like colonnades; a truly sumptuous medley of the noblest traditional forms.

A valet (it was you, Frankie, still just slim enough in those days to usher My Lady through a door) showed us to a drawing-room splendidly bristling with antlers and mounted otter heads. On a sofa beneath a large Gainsborough-style portrait of themselves in full hunting costume sat a young couple, the Gilliehursts.

Here we were at last, face-to-face with the only beings on earth who could save us from catastrophe. At that time they were still plain Mr and Mrs. Nevertheless, in a fit of sheer inspiration—extremity is surely the mother of invention—my wife conceived the brilliant notion, as we were introduced, of dropping a curtsey! Little Jean followed suit, plumb as if she had been rehearsed, and I, catching on in my slow way, did my best not to fumble a bow.

The Gilliehursts looked minutely startled, though I think you were not altogether displeased, were you, My Lady, nor you, My Lord. I think even then you had a proper enough sense of your own dignity to appreciate our spontaneous little offering.

Jean was led away by a matronly lady in a starched white coat, whom we took to be her future companion's nanny. It did cross my mind that Mrs Gilliehurst, with her beautiful, slim figure and her English-rose complexion (oh, indulge an old retainer, My Lady; his flattery is as harmless as it is sincere!), looked rather young to be the mother of a girl our Jean's age. But then maybe she wanted an older girl for her child, a sort of miniature duenna, perhaps. Anyway, knowing my daughter's charming nature, I was confident that she would lose no time in ingratiating herself with her new friend, whatever age she be.

While Jean was gone, my wife was given various secretarial tests, and I myself was questioned about our lives, habits, past, and so forth. As agreed upon earlier with my wife, I confessed my role in the Marquess of Avon fiasco (one never knew what inquiries might have been made), stressing my shame, and as it were throwing myself upon the Gilliehursts' clemency. Fortunately, Mr Gilliehurst's sense of humour was so robust— blessed man!—that he had long ago made up his mind that the whole affair was a most tremendous joke, even down to the Marquess's execution.

'They'll do as far as I'm concerned,' he snapped at last to his wife, and bounded off with deerstalker and Uzi, to hunt.

Now comes the delicate part of my story. After perhaps an hour had passed, and my wife had successfully demonstrated her skills to the Reeve, Jean was led back into the room. Mrs Gilliehurst excused herself for a moment and went off with the matron.

We soon realised our daughter was in a considerable state of distress. To our eager, whispered questions about her new companion, she responded with looks of heartbreakingly mute reproach. 'For heaven's sake, tell us what happened,' we urged her. She stared furiously at the ground, twisted one leg about the other in an appealingly coy way she had, then buried her head in her mother's skirts, muttering the word *trickle*.

Now, *trickle* was originally the word she had used in reference to the valve through which we trumpeters discharge the saliva that accumulates in our instruments—an operation Jean had always found so fascinatingly repulsive that by and by she had come to apply it to all the more intimate or embarrassing functions of her own body. Hearing her using a word with such connotations in these circumstances, we couldn't help but feel our parental instincts roused to a pitch of nervous alarm.

'Easy does it now,' I managed to mutter to my wife as Mrs Gilliehurst and the matron returned to the drawing-room. And to give my wife credit, she was practical even in her maternal indignation, taking care to address herself exclusively to the matron, as she asked waveringly, 'Would you mind telling me what you have been doing to my daughter?'

'Not at all, madam,' said the woman with a gentle smile that rather took the wind out of our sails. 'I was just examining her to make certain she was intact and hygienic. You'll be glad to hear that she is both.'

From indignation we were now plunged into blind bewilderment.

'What on earth do you need to know that for?' my wife asked, turning to Mrs Gilliehurst for enlightenment.

You coloured, My Lady; I think you even stamped your elegant foot! 'Well now really,' you said, 'I didn't imagine I was going to have to spell it out.'

But blusteringly, you did.

What bumpkins we were; what *provincials*. Still, the reader must remember that in those days the upper class's sensible practice of taking in young, undefiled girls from the lower orders (a rarity!) to bear their children when they, the girls, were of an age to do so, in order that their own womenfolk might be spared the tedium, labour, and loss of dignity, not to say figure, that pregnancy entails, was not yet nearly as widespread as it is today, and my wife and I had simply never come across it before. We would have liked, perhaps, a little more time to accustom ourselves to the idea than circumstances allowed.

'Well, I can't stand here all day waiting for your consent,' Mrs Gilliehurst said (the delicacy of the matter had made you a tiny bit peremptory with us, My Lady; quite understandable). 'You're perfectly free to leave if you don't like the idea.'

Perfectly free to leave! My wife and I looked at each other. Perhaps some last shred of something rippled out of our lives at that moment, though whatever it was has turned out to be dispensable, at least in my case. A moment later we were signing the necessary documents.

I date our time of happiness from that moment. Jean's and my own, at any rate. My wife fell into a mysterious decline which I am afraid to say affected her work, so that she was twice given formal warnings by the Reeve. Shortly after the second she disappeared from the estate, never, alas, to return. Jean, as I had predicted, rose sturdily to her new calling and, after two years' ripening, bore My Lady the first of four bonny infants, after which she was generously promoted to nursery maid with no further surrogation duties, though no sooner had she retired than she produced her own daughter, Molly (from whose strapping girth, Frankie, I think we know where to look for the paternity). Molly in her turn followed in her mother's honourable footsteps, bearing My Lady's daughter a healthy clutch of three. Sadly, she died of the third, but such is service, such is service.

As for myself, my duties have become pleasanter with every year that has passed. Factotum, Steward, Master of Ceremonies, and, pleasantest of all, bandleader to the Northumbria Yeomanry. Which reminds me, I must go and rehearse them for tomorrow's Ceremony of Good Air. A new tune has come into the official repertory for the event, or rather an old tune with a new name. What a triumphant reversal, what a stroke of political genius, to have taken at last the sting out of our enemies' still popular chant by using it to celebrate the very occasion of our National Pride! Certain disloyal subjects have apparently dared accuse our leaders of poor taste in this matter; have even, so I understand, published broadsheets satirising the noble ceremony itself. To them and their vile ilk let me repeat only the sacred words inscribed on the royal coat of arms of our illustrious House of Windsor: *Evil Be to Him Who Evil Thinks!*

# Spiders and Manatees

A familiar name appeared on the screen, above a little American flag. The figure in goggles and ski hat, crouching at the top of the jump slope, could of course be anybody. Still, Victoria peered forward, wondering whether she might glimpse some recognisable feature among the phosphorescent colours framed in her old television.

The figure launched himself onto the steep slope, elbows tight against his hips. His name still hung above him as he plunged towards the lip of the jump, and Victoria had a distinct memory of seeing it in a similar square-angled computer print at the top of a series of papers on Greek literature. Was this the same Carl Pepperall? His face was too masked, his body too crouched, for her to tell. She turned the volume knob, but the commentator must have fallen silent for the buildup to the jump. The figure gathered speed through the rush of static. A different camera showed him in profile slicing across the screen, and for the first time Victoria felt less than amused by the blotting-paper definition of her set. Could it be him? He hurtled down towards the lip and, with a final convulsion of his doubled-up body, took off into the lurid blue sky. But instead of turning into a sleek missile of compacted limbs and skis, he seemed to trip over some invisible rift in the air and open out into an ungainly assemblage of flailing, wheeling spindles that tumbled through the sky like an enormous daddy-longlegs.

Victoria watched askance as the man crashed to the ground and lay there in a heap, abruptly motionless, the unnatural colours of his ski clothes bleeding into the snow around him.

The commentator started to speak again, but Victoria lunged forward and turned off the television, wishing she had done so before the sports coverage had begun, though glad at least to have been quick enough to protect herself from a knowledge she did not wish to possess.

She took up her work again and edged herself back into the mood of delicate scorn with which she had been reviewing her old professor's latest offering on Epicharmus (how invigoratingly difficult it was to have a reputation for an unflinching critical eye!). The words flowed easily until, like a sudden *whump!* of oxygen into a smouldering fire, a glimpse of something vast, shadowy, and unnameable opened up in her.

The year before, Victoria had taken a teaching job at the small college of Branderhaven, in eastern Connecticut. From her classroom she could see across the campus to a buttressed Gothic fantasy that had been built to house what the prospectus described as a gym of unrivalled sophistication. It would already be full of students when she arrived to teach her morning class, and however late she left at night, there would still be dozens of young men and women exercising on the mysterious contraptions gleaming in the golden interior light.

*Occasionally they make a sortie*, she had written to her colleagues back in London, *for a lecture or seminar, but reluctantly, and you feel a little cruel dragging them away, even though it looks like a Bosch hell in there.* Mens sana *indeed. The faculty are the same. Not for them the salt of bracing interdisciplinary debate as seasoning to their (epicurean!)*

*lunches; no, any remarks that don't bear directly on the subject of fishing are considered practically scandalous. My contributions are lavish, as you can imagine. Do you remember Bill Platkin, the 'corn-fed Oklahoman'? The men are all like him, though the head of Humanities—a Hadley or Bradley—does show minute signs of life. He has offered to escort me around New York. No flowers please.*

A hard blue light was at work on the city, chiselling and bevelling angles, glazing planes. The cold sky looked packed with cut crystal. The place produced its customary effect on this latest initiate.

'It's like being inside a diamond,' Victoria announced. They passed a luminous violet tanning parlour, a shop selling the flowering parts of tropical plants. 'No, I'll tell you exactly what it's like, it's like a mixture of London, Rome, Madrid, and Venus.'

The brilliance of the morning and the affability of her companion had released a surge of effusive spirits in her, and she talked as she had not done since leaving London. Her phrases grew steadily pithier and more daring.

'There's a saurian strain to everything, even the people,' she informed the head of Humanities, Bradley Crane, who had obligingly agreed to show her Manhattan. 'They seem alert to different disturbances, do you know what I mean? As if they get their energies from different food sources. Any second now we're going to see a coiled tongue dart out to catch a fly.'

'Why, what are they eating in London these days?' Brad said, hoisting his amiably gloomy, hound-like jowls into a smile.

Victoria felt herself fuelled by his apparent pleasure. 'That car—it's like a hybrid of a Mercedes and an anaconda. What on earth is it?'

'Just a stretch limo.'

'A stretch limo! Even better!'

They were lunching in the West Village when Victoria, in full cry, experienced a distant pang of a kind she associated vaguely with the first suspicions of material loss—a lost wallet or set of keys. For a while the feeling hung in abeyance, unconnected with any discernible source. But its strength gathered until it made her falter mid-speech. The interruption seemed to startle Brad, and although he had shown no visible signs of inattention, he now smiled guiltily at Victoria, as if he had been caught drifting off. She resumed her flow, but in the fractional pause, her sense that she had been captivating this comfortable, weatherbeaten armchair of a man had already begun to cloud. When had she lost him? Had her appreciation of his city been too pert for his liking? A few days ago he had seemed like one of those miracles that arrive in your life so matter-of-factly you hardly remember the anguish, the aridity, that preceded them. The smell of his big, damp sheepskin coat had intimated such vastnesses of friendship and repose. Surely she couldn't have been mistaken. She could feel a shrillness in her voice. She suspected she ought to be quiet, stopped talking for a moment, but Brad said nothing, and the silence pushed them apart like a spreading pool. An ill-looking man went by the window leading a poodle with a bondage stud collar.

'Enter the age of sex by proxy,' Victoria said with a little laugh.

Brad smiled, but seemed unamused. Or was she imagining things? She tried again, but all her words came out off-colour or faintly condescending, and she wished she could shut up. But the more she felt herself grating on Brad, the more she felt it imperative to regain his attention. As they left the restaurant, she gave a rendering of her dinner with the dean on her first night in Branderhaven, roguishly quoting the catch-phrases that had been bandied about, the *hidden agendas*, *significant others*, 'Oh, and yes, Brad, *serendipitous moments*, I counted three *serendipiti* . . . ' But he wasn't to be tempted into the cosiness of a secret conspiracy, and his non-committal, barely audible response made her feel shallow and treacherous; 'You mustn't think I'm being disloyal, now,' but that only made it worse . . .

All the while, however, she retained a provisional quality in these feelings. She was quite possibly imagining things; one was seldom anywhere near as awful as one feared.

In a tunnel of the Fourteenth Street IRT subway station, they turned a corner and came face to face with a man defecating. The man stared at them brazenly, furiously, from the ghetto of his hood. As they passed by, Victoria began to say something—not, as it happened, anything to do with the man—but Brad silenced her unceremoniously with an abrupt, upward gesture of the back of his hand.

'I mean,' he said, at once conciliatory, 'I guess that doesn't require any comment.'

Victoria was too crushed to explain that she had actually been about to ask him if he had ever taken a Mediterranean Antiquities Cruise.

There were tulips on her desk the next morning, white ones with feathery waves bred into the curl. She recognised them vaguely, but couldn't remember where from. There was no note. Brad? It seemed unlikely after the silent, humiliating train journey home last night. But there they were—white, fresh, cleansing the air about them. Perhaps Bradley was one of those men who have to insult you as a way of testing their own feelings. She smiled. She was not averse to the idea of a little combative wooing.

Her performance in class that morning was freer and lighter than usual, leavened by her secret excitement. At one point, several students spontaneously began taking notes—a sight that was always astonishing and gratifying. Even the curly-haired, track-suited Carl Pepperall, who sat at the back in a permanent foment of suppressed calisthenics, was unusually attentive. He was gazing at her with a look of shy wonder. Had his ears been opened at last to the riches of Greek verse? She asked his opinion of a Sapphic conceit. A panicky look came over him. She smiled and asked another student. A breath of the tulip fragrance sent a flutter of delicate apprehension through her.

After the class she made straight for the faculty building. Ita, Brad's Maltese secretary, eating a Danish pastry from a box in which glistened several more, gave her a grin and asked how she'd enjoyed New York. Victoria thought she detected a trace of archness in the woman's voice, though it was hard to tell with the chomping and swallowing going on.

'It was very pleasant, thank you.'

'Bradley sure enjoyed himself.'

'Did he?'

'Sure!' *Shewer*, Ita bellowed it with a shower of crumbs and a rolling of eyes, as if her word had been doubted. She put a finger to her chin, tilted her head, and stared.

Victoria had attempted to make a motherly confidante of this woman, but there was something not quite satisfactorily maternal about her, despite her bun of silver hair and the voluminous softness of her figure. She was oddly dilatory over the small administrative matters Victoria had asked her to settle, and she was prone to quirky sulks.

She pointed at the door to Brad's office and said with a little twinkle, 'He's in there now,' as if Victoria's single thought had been emblazoned on her forehead.

In fact, the woman's peculiar clairvoyance disarmed Victoria to the extent that she found herself opening Brad's door in a state of dreamy suggestibility, without even stopping to think of an excuse. Brad was lounging back with his feet on the desk and fiddling with a quiver of small, brightly coloured feathers. He glanced up.

'Hi, Victoria. What can I do for you?'

Victoria faltered. Brad began to wind thread about the feathers while she tried to think of something. His hands were absolutely steady. He did not have the air of a man who had just sent an anonymous gift of fancy tulips.

'I wanted to thank you for a lovely time yesterday,' Victoria improvised.

Brad gave her an empty look.

'Oh, sure.'

She stood helplessly. She felt mortified, but she couldn't bring herself to leave. She watched herself in horror as she stepped forward and touched the little posy of feathers in Brad's hand.

'It's pretty, what is it?' she said.

Then she felt something prick her, and simultaneously heard Brad roar 'Fly', or seem to, making the word sound so much more like a command than an answer that she jumped back and fled from the room, smarting.

Ita avoided her eye, busying herself with a sticky finger, a look of sly, sullen amusement on her face.

For a few days Victoria made efforts to find out who her anonymous admirer was. Men who were courteous enough to sit next to her at lunch or say hello to her in the faculty building found themselves at the receiving end of alarmingly piercing looks, which in no time had them retreating into the iciest of professional formalities.

A whisper of quiet panic began to greet her wherever she went. She was too shrewd not to notice the rout—the contortions of evasive behaviour; eyes beseeching rescue, midsentence flights for forgotten books, the quick getaways made under cover of a dazzling smile . . .

She realised she had better get a grip on herself. *Anyone would think I came here to get a husband*, she wrote to her old colleagues, and she resolved to cut a figure of dignified

81

aloofness in the remaining months of her appointment. She dropped her investigation and, in a mood of combined pique and defiance, withdrew from Branderhaven's small social arena. *If they choose to see me as an academic* Gastarbeiter *imported from a nation fallen on hard times, then far be it from me to embarrass them with social obligations. I shall henceforth conduct myself with the meekness of a governess in a nineteenth-century novel* . . .

She applied herself to her classes with added diligence, spending long hours preparing intricate summaries and appraisals, going through the students' papers with an attention vastly out of proportion to anything that had gone into their making. She ate lunch at a table on her own unless she was specifically invited to join the others, which happened rarely, then not at all. And at night she retired early, proudly, with a Sanskrit primer.

The magnolia flowered hard and bright all over the campus. A week later it fell and the ground was covered with drifts of rotting blossom. An early summer brought the class out in silks and pastels. Music came on the breeze from the steps to the gym, where the students gathered in the warm, lengthening evenings. Victoria watched them as she worked at her desk. They strolled out of the big glass doors in loose tunics and togas, a little more glowing flesh on show every night. *It's the Baths of Caracalla over there*, Victoria wrote, *soon we'll be down to thongs and loincloths* . . .

Bradley receded into the background. There remained something silently contemptuous about his presence whenever it encroached on her horizon, but he was not difficult to avoid. She seldom thought of the white tulips now, remembering them merely as an irritatingly mysterious interruption of her life's natural medium, like a blizzard in a desert. Stoicism and work were to form her natural continuity. She pledged herself to them with a fierceness that was intended to purge every other inclination from her heart.

One evening she was making notes for a class on Greek metrics when her concentration—usually excellent—began to stray and would not be brought to heel. She had long ago discovered the flagellant's secret of control, which is to make things harder when they are hard, rather than easier. She turned from the notes to the more arduous task of memorising another passage of Homer (she had resolved to learn the *Odyssey* by heart before her thirty-fifth birthday). When that didn't work, she pulled a newspaper from her bag, picked a column at random, and began translating it into Greek, an exercise she relished for its sublime purity of purpose.

She had worked herself into a cold blaze of effort searching the ancient language for epithets that would do justice to a modern fashion article (in what terms would Pericles' Athenians have conceived of Day-Glo and mohair, of spandex, chenille, and distressed leather?) when the door opened and the barefooted figure of Carl Pepperall appeared inside the classroom.

He looked at her silently for a moment. He seemed very far away, obscured in a tissue of soft sounds and night scents that had trailed in with him, and then further removed by an afterswirl of dictionary print milling before her eyes like a gnat cloud. She heard him speak—'Oh, excuse me, ma'am'—and had the odd impression of seeing his lips move out of time with his words. 'I think I left my sneakers in here.' He rummaged for them under the table, stood up, and grinned at her. She hoped he would go now. She was aware of him peering at her, and of herself sitting there without speaking or moving. She must have been straining her eyes. The room looked very dark, and everything in it seemed to pulse. Light dissolved from the boy as if he were a body of light steeped in dark water.

'Are you all right?' she heard him say. The words seemed spoken in a foreign tongue. He was approaching, a look of concern on his face. She had an urge to hide the work she was doing, but her limbs felt too heavy to move. He stood by her, looking down at the desk. Her forehead tingled coldly, as if at the onset of fear.

'You're translating the *Times* into Greek,' he said; 'what are you doing that for?'

She could hardly look at him, let alone answer his question. Her head was bowed in shame. After a moment's silence he gave an unexpectedly assured chuckle. 'Why don't you take a break?' he asked. 'Come over to the gym.'

She was on a walkway above an echoing, cathedral-like space lit so brilliantly she was at first aware only of a multiplying gleam of chrome and glass and polished wood. She had been led there in what amounted to a state of suspended volition. Protests and practicalities had crumbled in the face of Carl's polite, confident insistence. (Where had he got that sudden flow of confidence from—her own ebb? Some power source unknown to her?) Her glimpses through the windows of the gym had not prepared her for the size of the interior. She remembered her arrival in New York. Here was the same dazzle, the same power of pure scale: a broad central aisle given over to game after game of basketball and tennis; glass-partitioned votive chapels full of weight-lifters, masked fencers, squash players hurling themselves at walls like flies in a jar; a huge blue swimming pool scribbled over with glyphs of gold light (the ringing air above it somehow darker and more solemn than elsewhere). The locker room, where she changed into a borrowed tracksuit, had a primary, carnal reek. How odd it felt to be back where the body was the measure and arbiter of reality. She had seldom ventured into this empire since childhood.

She met Carl by the aerobics machines.

'We'll start with some stretching,' he said. 'If you just copy me . . .'

She allowed her gaze to settle squarely on his body for the first time. There was an unsightly scar—a livid rose—at the back of his thigh, but otherwise she had to concede that he looked as a human male was probably intended to look. The few others she had eyed with the same licence were spiders or manatees in comparison. A smooth plait of muscle was visible under his string vest, which flowed like chain-mail over the burl of his shoulders as he plunged forward on alternate knees.

Victoria sounded herself for a reaction. Was she impressed? Amused? (What would her old colleagues think if they could see her with him like this?) Ignited? None of these exactly, though when he turned to smile silently after the receding figure of a girl with a Walkman, in a tight, metallic-green leotard, who had flipped him with her towel as she went by, Victoria felt the lapse of attention like the chill of a sudden draught.

'What did you do to your leg?' she asked.

He turned his attention back to her.

'Propeller got me. I fell out of a boat in a power race off Virginia Beach.' He grinned. 'I have a lot of them. They're my souvenirs. Here, harpoon dart from the Caribbean, St Croix.' He showed her a sheeny white gouge in his shoulder, then touched his hip. 'Got a steel pin in there from a hang-gliding fall. The wind decided to drop just as I did. That was in northern Spain, Asturias Mountains. My mom swears she dies every time the phone rings when I'm off on a trip . . .'

There was something touching about the unembarrassed, intimate disclosures. He seemed to take a guileless pleasure in fixing her attention on his body. Without noticing the point of transition in her own thoughts, she found herself trying to picture him stealing through the icy fog of a March dawn with a bunch of white tulips in his hand. She looked at him afresh. The image shimmered in and out of plausibility. There seemed all at once an irresistible hint of affinity between the flowers and the boy's fair curls and limbs gleaming in the neon light. If he had been a god visiting a mortal in a dream, Victoria reflected, he might have left such flowers as his tokens of remembrance. She smiled, and tried to shrug off the idea; the boy must be more than ten years younger than herself.

'Now we'll try the machines,' he said.

He sat her on a bicycle and explained the principles of aerobics. He was standing beside her, just outside her field of vision, so that he was both looming and abstract. His voice was impassively polite, like an airline steward's. It was difficult to get any purchase on him, or on her relation to him, now that they were outside the simple geometries of the classroom, and now that the spectre of the tulips had risen again in her mind. She didn't know whether to feel flattered or obscurely insulted by the way he was ordering her around. Then too, she thought now, there was the matter of his papers—those punctual, immaculately presented reports on classical litera-ture that arrived on her desk like lambs to the slaughter, so virginally innocent were they of anything approaching origi-nality or even cogency. The students were graded at the end of the semester, and in all conscience it was going to be difficult to award Carl anything more than a bare minimum 'pass'. It would be a pity if he should think he had done anything to make her vindictive. Awkward too. It crossed her mind that she might have been incautious coming here with one of her students. A delicate suggestion of impropriety flittered through the air. She didn't know what to do. She didn't even know what she wanted to do. The situation seemed globed in a complex burnish, like that of a vase under several layers of glaze, with a dozen different shades and hues. And at the point where her own feelings might have been expected to guide her, the shades merely deepened to a pitch of absolute mysteriousness.

Without warning, Carl touched her throat. As it turned out,

he was only taking her pulse, but it felt like a detonation, and in the few silent seconds in which he let his fingertips rest near her jugular, her blood seemed to perform a drumroll right beneath them, and in her agitation she pedalled furiously, as if trying to reach a speed that would persuade the fixed machine to move.

'You probably should exercise more,' Carl said, and prescribed ten minutes each of cycling and rowing.

She sat on a ledge in the women's steam-bath, stupefied by pain and exhaustion. *See you later*, Carl had said. Did that mean goodbye or later on this evening?

At first, on the bicycle, the extreme physical effort had been an adventure, and she had reported on it to Carl in her customary style. 'I feel like a maternity ward for newborn muscles screaming into life,' she had informed him, and 'The more pain you're in, the longer each second on the stopwatch seems to last. There must be a point of convergence between absolute agony and eternity. I suppose that's where hell is.'

But at a certain level of exhaustion, her body had begun to reel her mind in like a kite, until it was wrapped so closely about her limbs it seemed merely a dim radiance from them, barely distinguishable from the sweat and heat. No more thoughts occurred in it, only the notation of strain and lung-burn, and the wish to stop.

'I can't do any more,' she gasped after the first ten minutes.

'Quick,' Carl said, 'it's important to keep your pulse up.' He led her to the rowing machine, and was strapping her feet to the boards, heedless of her protests.

'Now pull.' It seemed she must.

The seat slid back on the horizontal spine as she dragged at the weighted chain, her feet braced against the boards. The chain drove a geared bicycle wheel with flaps fixed all around it, which fanned her as she sweated. Carl stood over her, again a little behind, issuing curt instructions—*A little faster, pull harder now, keep that speed up . . .*

A pattern had emerged: she would reach a peak of agony, slacken, be admonished, protest she had had enough, then feel a downsurge of shadow as Carl leaned forward, an indistinct mass of male form, to touch her throat. And once she had discovered the degree of protest that would bring him, she had half-consciously summoned him, as one does summon again and again the thing that most perplexes. She still wasn't sure what it was his touch induced. It felt like a panicky lurch, as over a forgotten step, or perhaps more like the lurch from a step that isn't there. It was always this way in matters of physical experience; one was more than ever the proverbial Greek in Rome: a creature of refinement thronged by the unpredictable barbarians of appetite. One never quite knew what was going on. A limitless, treacherous obscurity would open up, accompanied by a feeling of helplessness that kept her to the task. She was only capable of doing what she was told. She recognised the feeling from three or four other occasions in her adult life—the same unaccountable surrender, the same excruciating pain, the same blind obligation to go through with it.

'Okay,' he said at last. 'You can stop now.'

She lay prone, awaiting further instructions. But he was already leaving.

'See you later,' he said with a smile, and was gone.

Now what? A drama of folly seemed to be unfolding in some shadowy zone between the real and the imaginary. How would it proceed, she wondered: towards a moonlit confession under the magnolias? A silent entanglement in the locked classroom? She felt quite numb towards the eventualities, as if she too were suspended in that indeterminate zone. The steam appeared to have dissolved her skin. It swirled and bloomed inside her. Blurred pink figures moved softly around the room.

And then a paler one came in and sat down opposite. It was the girl in the Walkman and tight green leotard she had seen earlier on, the girl who had flipped Carl with her towel. Her skin was almost as white as the steam-room's porcelain tiles, which boosted the bits of colour on her. She swept back a damp mass of reddish ringlets, yawned, wrinkled her nose, and gazed into the steam with a look of self-satisfaction.

But before that, her eyes had flickered briefly over Victoria's, and in the instant the older woman had felt the ripple of banished illusion. One flickering look and it was gone! She wondered at her capacity for missing the obvious. How could she have imagined Carl would be remotely interested in herself when a creature like this was at his disposal? It wasn't as if she had even desired the things she had imagined, unless a weakness for the flattery of being desired be itself considered a desire. If she felt anything now, it was more like relief for what she had been spared.

How familiar this turn of events felt. Fantasy, disillusion, relief: the cycle seemed peculiarly her own. Even when the fantasy happened by chance to land her in a grapple with one of those spiders or manatees, there would always be a moment when something rock-like reared up with an unarguable veto to any pleasure she might have had from it, and in retrospect this moment would always seem one of deliverance. It had even been so, she realised, with Bradley, after that day in New York. She had been too preoccupied with her humiliation to notice it at the time, but after it was all over, something in her had breathed an unmistakable sigh of relief.

Meanwhile, as she looked at the girl, she could feel the knotted burden of Carl, and the tulips, and the strain of over-work unravelling, and it was like a physical sensation of loosening in her body.

Gradually, a mood of benign calm settled on her. She smiled ruefully to herself, thinking of Carl and the girl together—an affinity of toned flesh. She felt an almost protective magnanimity, as if she were an old priestess presiding over their nuptials. Steam made the blood tingle in her capillaries. She had never known anything quite so luxurious as this steamroom; one felt almost afloat in the assuaging cloud. She stared at the girl, glazed in good feeling. It wasn't often that she was able to forget herself in this way. She wondered whether the supposedly warmer, more candid palette of American emotion was at last beginning to colour her own feelings. Waves of tenderness seemed to be pulsing out of her.

The girl caught her eye—a green glint—then looked away. Pink blotches had appeared on her skin. The corners of her dark red lips were drawn up further, and to a finer point than most, as if they had been detailed by an unusually expert hand. How nice she would look if she smiled. Victoria found herself feeling extraordinarily well-disposed towards the girl, towards everything! It seemed to her inexpressibly wonderful that Carl and the girl should be lovers. She smiled, picturing them together. The steam plumed obligingly into boas, bulged into pillows and glistening cherub clusters. Again the girl caught her eye, and it was like a splash of sea-green against the portholes of a sinking ship. How delightful to sink like this: into a whirlpool of soft contours, mild brush-strokes of bluish shadow, steam-darkened braids and knots of copper . . . Victoria had always considered any form of body fascination to be infantile. She refused to read certain novels: *boredom not prudishness*, she would tell people; *it's like having a travel book that does nothing but tell you about the workings of the car.* And even now she had a suspicion that she ought not to indulge these feelings. But where was the harm? His hand would descend through the meadow of freckles sloping from each sunburned shoulder to an areola ringed, she noticed, with dainty marks that might have been cast from the paw-prints of a thimble-sized lion. She imagined the contact of hand and breast. Another green wave crashed as something exulted in her blood.

'Jesus!' the girl exploded, and jumped up, covering herself with her hands. She spat out another word as she left the room. Victoria coiled as it tore into her, bulleting through what seemed like a series of opaque veils through which she was able to glimpse briefly the source of her imagined exultation . . . The glimpse faded as the rips healed, though she was not altogether spared the knowledge, because in the flurry of violation something brilliant and silken had rippled out of her memory, and to her astonishment she was seeing a vase of those white, feathery tulips in the faculty room at the very beginning of the semester, an overheard voice saying, *Yes, they're pretty, my neighbour gives them to me, he's a commercial breeder*; the voice female, accented, muffled by sounds of chewing and salivation.

It took a few days for the glare of revelation to fade. Something in the mixture of cruelty and craving in Ita's gesture gave it a certain lingering fascination. But eventually Victoria was able to consign the image and all it insinuated back to the darkness from which it had arisen. A sense of having in an obscure way been made a fool of was all that remained of the episode.

Was this what her Greeks thought of as *Ananke*: necessity; the force that draws all things forward to their designated place, do what they might to resist it, so that even one's defiance of its decrees is taken into account?

A day of blinding sunshine . . . the shadow-etched campus emptied for some annual, end-of-semester joust between seniors and alumni . . . cries drifting over from the sports field behind the gym . . . Victoria was clearing out her desk in the classroom when a woman knocked on the open door and strolled in. She took off a pair of sunglasses. She was handsome, clear-skinned, her blond hair grained with grey; blue eyes that appeared lit from the back with mauve. She smiled at Victoria, extending a hand.

'Hi. I'm Sophie Pepperall. I think you know my son.'

What followed had a dream-like, faintly incredible quality, even at the time. The woman had stood before her, pleading for her son, though pleading was not quite the word, as she seemed sure of getting what she wanted, as if she were going through the motions of an elaborate ritual, purely out of some vague nostalgia for more courtly times. She was relaxed, almost playful, sunglasses dangling from one hand, the other trespassing lightly and confidently on Victoria's arm.

Her gist was that Carl's place at the business school his father had attended was contingent on a grade average that he might have scraped if he hadn't done so badly in Victoria's class.

'It's not a particularly high average they're looking for,' Mrs Pepperall explained, 'but on the other hand they don't appear to have too much flexibility.' She paused for a moment, smiling at Victoria. 'Bradley Crane told me it was unusual for a student to get a grade that low, especially in this kind of subject . . .' She looked at Victoria candidly, leaving the pleasant spill of colour from her eyes to express the thing that even her idea of propriety stopped her from saying. Carl's face stared out from hers, boyish and vulnerable beneath her confident smile.

Victoria remembered the acute discomfort she had felt as she answered the woman—the astonishment at what was being asked of her, the desire not to betray the angry thudding of her heart, to sound measured, reasonable, in perfect command of herself . . . It had taken several very painful minutes to convince the woman that her decision was a solid, objective fact and not open to negotiation.

She was still recovering from the effort a few minutes later when Brad strode in without knocking. He was carrying the computer print-out of the student grades, and he looked more dour than Victoria had ever seen him.

'I'd like you to reconsider this now,' he said, holding the print-out towards Victoria.

She tried to keep her voice steady. 'I've just been asked to reconsider it by his mother.'

'Yes, and now I'd like to ask you again.' It seemed he had thrust a pen into her hand, which was poised above the print-out. He stood waiting, his expression stiff and remote.

'I'm afraid it's out of the question,' she heard herself say.

It was more a matter of *can't* than *won't*; a sense of almost physiological impossibility, like a fish being asked to breathe air.

'You can change it yourself, though, if you want to. I won't tell anyone.'

She flinched as if from an expected blow, as Brad leaned over the desk towards her and snatched the pen back from her hand.

He folded up the print-out.

'Very amusing,' he said, and walked out, leaving her with a sense of victory which even at the time felt curiously incomplete.

She sat in the wintry shadows of her flat, facing the darkened screen of the television, where the figure had tripped and lurched and spun out of control. For a moment she felt an urge to switch the set on again, not that the programme was likely to be on the same subject any longer. But even suppose it was, she told herself, and suppose the figure was indeed her Carl Pepperall, and suppose, purely for the sake of hypothesis, that something unpleasant had happened to him; what did any of that have to do with her? She assured herself that she had done nothing to be ashamed of, that she had acted out of the same high, unflinching principle as she was now bringing to her old professor's book on Epicharmus. In the end one could only shrug and dismiss the episode, if there even was an episode, as a grotesque coincidence of the kind that life occasionally throws up in imitation of those engineered by the lesser tragedians. It would be a mistake to look for any meaning in it. She switched on a light and returned to her review.

But she was in tumult. She saw the white tulips again, the treacherous steam, and the vibrant white blur of mountainside with the body sprawled on it. She saw the mother again, and the son's face buried in her features. A tremor went through her. She sensed briefly the cold touch of eternity that had used her intricate, coiled-up soul as its instrument, and felt how exquisitely it had fingered the keys.

# Macrobiotic

A s I opened the door to Lorrie's apartment, I heard a familiar voice from inside. Roy Mulroney, my predecessor in Lorrie's affections, was on the sofa that backed against the bar dividing the living-room from the kitchen.

He rose to greet me, his gangly frame reaching into the upper shadows of the room.

'Hi, Phil. How're you doing?' He shook my hand and seemed to want to clap my shoulder.

'Good to see you,' he said instead.

He was wearing jeans, a thick plaid shirt, and the scuffed brown leather jacket that gave a slight acrid reek of horse and saddlery whenever he moved.

'How's it going?' I asked him.

'Hey, can't complain. How about you?'

'Good. Pretty good.'

He smiled, his blue eyes looking at me with their sparkle of faint rakishness.

I smiled back at him.

Lorrie's slender hands were dicing vegetables on the wooden bar-top behind him. Their owner's head was hidden by the row of cabinets running across the ceiling. In the kitchen's heightened gleam, their graceful movements gave them the look of a pair of eerily articulated marionettes on a miniature stage. I stared at them for a moment, struck by how beautiful they were: small and long-fingered, the slimly tapered upper joints bent back a little as if unusually pliant, the nails fluted. Wet carrots and daikon lay in ruins beside them. I went round the bar. Lorrie finished chopping a bunch of bok choy before turning to me.

She was wearing the soft, leaf-patterned blue kimono that she sometimes used as a bathrobe. I stepped forward to kiss her. She put the heels of her hands on my hips, holding me at arm's length, and gave me a kiss: a cool kiss.

'I'm all sweaty,' she explained. 'Roy showed up just when I was about to take a shower.'

She looked up at me, her eyes staring into mine. She seemed to be straining towards me, as if from behind a barrier of her own, or against one of mine. I didn't know if this glaze-like effect represented something real or a figment of my imagination, but this was not the first time I had felt its presence.

I relieved her at the chopping board so that she could go and have her shower. I tried to remember which was the right way to chop the vegetables in order to focus their nutritive powers as Lorrie had taught me.

Roy sat on the sofa, his sprawled frame twisted round to face me.

He and Lorrie had lived together in Colorado and Montana for seven years. After that they had come to New York, where they had broken up; Lorrie had got pregnant, and they had decided not to keep the child. Roy had been out of the country when I met Lorrie, and by the time he returned to New York he was with another woman.

While Lorrie was in the shower he repeated to me the conversation he and Lorrie had been having before I arrived. They had been discussing whether or not to see a film that night, and if so which one. He repeated the discussion almost verbatim. They hadn't been able to agree on a film, and as I listened I could hear their quarrel as if it were happening right there in front of me.

'So I tell her, Why don't we let Phil decide, honey; that'd be fairest, wouldn't it? And she goes, No, it wouldn't, so I say, Look, honey—'

I interrupted him: 'Let's see the documentary.'

After a momentary pause he gave a smile.

'That's what I wanted to hear, Phil.' He thumped his knee with an outspread hand (the unnaturally large finger-span gave it a shaggy look, adding to an overall impression of upright wolf). Then he stood and shouted down the corridor, 'Phil wants to see the documentary. You hear that, honey?' Getting no answer from the drumming bathroom, he turned to me, saying, 'Be right back.' He went down the short corridor and stood outside the bathroom door.

'Honey, you catch that? Phil says no to the schlock.'

'Can't hear you' came Lorric's shower-muffled voice.

He shouted again and there was the same muffled response.

I could just see to the end of the corridor from where I stood at the chopping board. I tried to induce a feeling of calm indifference to what I sensed was going to happen. I opened a container of bean curd and took the white, flabby brick from its clouded waters. I heard Roy mutter 'Hell' and saw his great hand go to the handle of the bathroom door. He turned the handle and let himself in. The shower noise jumped in volume. I leaned on the wooden bar-top and heard them shouting at each other. Bantering abuse; old lovers' routines. The bean curd fell into soft, jellyish segments under my blade. I tumbled the chopped carrot and daikon into the steel steaming basket and put it into the seething water on the stove. I looked for Lorrie's voice in my mind and heard it tell me not to be ruled by the primitive feeling that had begun to rise in me. What did it mean for her to be standing naked in front of the man she had slept with for eight years? Nothing. She meant no more to him naked than she did clothed. The only harm would be in pretending there was something wrong when there wasn't. That would be English and this was America. That would be the past and this was the future. I tried to concentrate on the cooking, but after a moment I found myself picturing her there in front of him in the glassy bathroom light; her tall, rangy body a little blurred by the steam and the shower curtain, the water darkening her fair hair, bringing a flush of blood to her cheeks and shallow breasts, streaming around her hips and thighs. A feeling that was like being burned on the inside with a cold flame came into me. I told myself that what I was experiencing was an irrelevance, a throwback, a superstition. After a few moments it would pass, and then I would feel all right again, unless I gave in to it first and stormed down the corridor as a part of me wanted to, in which case I would spend the rest of the evening regretting it.

Roy padded back in, with a look of satisfaction.

'Bitch tried to put up a fight, but I wore her down.'

I turned from him and checked the vegetables. Steam mushroomed in my face.

'Everything okay there, Phil?'

I stood at the stove with my back to him. Before me were the roots steaming in their steel pot, the greens and bean curd waiting to be added, the brown rice bubbling. Beside and above were Lorrie's supplies of dried kombu seaweed and bancha twigs, tubbed miso, umeboshi paste, tempeh, seitan.

'Something the matter there?' I heard Roy ask.

The amicable tone of his voice seemed to come at me from a future I hadn't quite caught up with but soon would. I turned back to face him. I sensed that in my position it would not have crossed his mind to be disturbed by what had happened. He would not have comprehended these feelings. Their function was archaic, prehistoric, and their survival in my own psyche was an anachronism. I thought of this and it seemed to calm me.

'Everything okay?' Roy asked.

I nodded, but when I opened my mouth I felt a constriction in my throat and I didn't trust myself to speak. Roy looked puzzled, then concerned. I stood with my mouth open.

'You all right there, Phil?' Roy asked. 'Everything okay?'

I nodded again. The feeling of a cold flame passed out of my body. It seemed to me that any moment soon I would be able to say something calm and perfectly friendly.

# The Volunteer

There was a new resident at the shelter. She was small and bony, with dark, olive-coloured skin. Her face was a little puffy, which might have been from bruises, or prolonged sleeplessness, or dissipation of one kind or another. She wore a tracksuit of faded mauve cotton, with frayed drawstrings dangling from the hood and elastic cuffs that looked as if they had been nibbled at by mice. Her eyes were narrow and pretty, scimitar-shaped slits with yellowish brown pupils and unhealthily discoloured whites. The lashes were soft and curled, and she had emphasised them with makeup, a striking contrast to her otherwise drab appearance. Her name was Tina.

The shelter was in the crypt of St Ursula's, a Catholic church in the part of Manhattan called Alphabet City. It consisted of a long, raftered, stone-floored gallery, with bathrooms, a kitchen, and a TV room off to the side. There were statuary cornices under the rafters and a few crayon Sunday-school pictures on the walls; but the windowless, overheated space was not especially pleasant, and it was up to the residents themselves to make the atmosphere congenial.

There was room for fourteen residents, male and female. They and the night's volunteer ate a communal meal at a refectory table in the kitchen, cooking and cleaning up by roster. Afterwards they would chat or watch television, drinking coffee and turning the unventilated air blue with cigarette smoke. At a quarter past ten they wheeled out the folded, prison-built beds and set them up in the long gallery; men at one end, women at the other.

We, the volunteers, had a curtained-off annexe to ourselves, at the bottom of a ramp that led up from the crypt to the main body of the church itself. We slept on the same uncomfortable beds as the residents: short, with thin, slippery, plastic-covered mattresses that didn't hold the sheets.

I had been working as a volunteer at the shelter once a week for two months, and I was now considered trained, which meant that I didn't need another volunteer to work with me. Our job was to let in the residents at seven-thirty in the evening, open locked store cupboards if extra supplies were needed, turn out the lights at ten-thirty, and make sure everyone was gone by seven in the morning. If an argument broke out we were expected to settle it, or get help if we couldn't; if a resident turned up showing signs of intoxication of any kind, we were supposed to send him or her away. In practice such occurrences were virtually unheard of: the residents were screened before being referred to the shelter, and quite apart from it being in their interest to keep the place in good order, they were aware of what expulsion meant. Several of them had spent time at the city's public shelters, and what they said confirmed all the worst rumours of squalor and violence in circulation at that time.

Our role was largely symbolic, then: we represented the domiciled among the homeless, and this gave us our authority. Because of the kind of people we were, and because almost nothing untoward ever occurred, we carried this authority awkwardly, like a burden, and tended to compensate for it with an exaggerated humility, an overeager solicitousness with the residents, which made relations with them intricate and sometimes anxious. I was no exception in this.

Nevertheless, in my two months there, I had become attached to the place. I got on well with most of the residents, and I had even become fond of the physical surroundings. The metal cupboards and calcium-bearded radiators; the soiled woollen curtains dividing off the volunteers' annexe (the wool itself like carded dust); the bits of carpet remnant in the TV room; the opaque lamp globes, each with a fuzz of city soot like a shaven head; the refectory table in its sticky sweat of wax: the whole dingy, grimed-over place, with its almost human air of shrugging unillusion, had become familiar to me and unexpectedly comforting.

Almost as soon as we sat down to dinner I saw that Tina, the new resident, had not settled in.

The communal meal was the focal point of the evening; for many residents undoubtedly the highlight of their day. From my first visit, I had been struck by the warmth and liveliness of the occasion: these were people who had been exposed to prolonged and quite extraordinary hardship, but between what for many of them were the more or less blank hours of daytime wandering and the oblivion of sleep, against the bare surroundings of the shelter itself, an atmosphere of surprising cheerfulness and neighbourly goodwill flourished for an hour or so each evening.

It was here that the more extrovert among the residents came into their own: Subalowsky with his wheezy chest and paralysed hand; Pam, young, acne-scarred, with her candid but strangely impersonal descriptions of her counselling sessions and Antabuse treatment; Selwyn from Arkansas, always stylishly turned out, flamboyant, with an exaggerated courtesy in all his gestures; Lucky with her boxer's black eyes, cropped hair, white stubble on her chin, and raucous laugh that retroactively turned anything that prompted it into a dirty joke . . . The talkers talked, but the shyer, more dazed or withdrawn were also included in the general current of conviviality. They par-

ticipated quietly, with sympathetic smiles or other small gestures of attentiveness, and even the most depressed among
them would seem briefly distracted from their problems.

Tina, however, the newcomer, appeared to be making little
effort to enter into this spirit. If anything, she seemed to be
keeping herself deliberately aloof. She sat a little back from
the table, holding her plate in her lap and concentrating on
it with a severe, preoccupied look. I saw that most of the people
talking attempted to include her in their audience, though
even then, still relatively soon after she had first come to the
shelter, there was a noticeable hesitancy in their gaze as it
settled on her, as if she had already accustomed them to having
their attentions rebuffed.

At one point she turned conspicuously in my direction.
Selwyn was joking about his attempts to join the National
Guard in Arkansas.

'I said I wanted to be the first Negro married to a President
of the United States. Apparently I had the wrong attitude . . .'

While he was talking Tina caught my eye with a distinctly
contemptuous look in her own. It was as if some lofty and
scornful pact existed between us. Other residents noticed this
and watched for my reaction. I had hardly spoken a word to
Tina so far, and her gesture—unaccountable, oddly decisive
in its execution, impossible to ignore—took me by surprise.
Aware of the delicacy of my position, wishing neither to snub
the newcomer nor to offend Selwyn, I assumed a diplomati-
cally abstracted look, and the small tension of the moment
passed. However, it left me with the impression of a strong
and not very likeable personality.

The following week Tina gave me a grin as she came through
the entrance of the shelter.

'Hello, Simon.'

She was carrying an empty-looking valise. I noticed a jerkiness in the way she walked, a faint, puppet-like tottering
movement in each step.

While dinner was being prepared she stood near me, as if
she wanted to talk. I gave her my volunteer's smile, and she
sat down next to me at the refectory table, where I was shred-
ding lettuce on a chopping board. She pulled her chair close
to mine, glancing around at the other people in the kitchen.
When she spoke, it was in a low, whispery voice, so that I
had to lean towards her in order to follow. As I did, I caught
a musty smell of sandalwood.

'So, Simon, you having a good time?'

'Yes, thank you. Are you?'

'You been working here long?'

'Two months. A little over.'

'How old you are?'

'I'm thirty.'

'You from Europe or someplace, right?'

'My mother's English. I used to live in England.'

'What's your other name?'

I told her my surname.

'What name is that?'

'It's Jewish, if that's what you mean.'

'How long you been in this country, Simon?'

'Two years, on and off.'

'You like it?'

'On the whole. What about you, do you like it?'

'You got family over here, right?'

'Hey, Tina'—this was Selwyn, laying the table with the
kitchen's yellowing silverware and unbreakable plastic plates
—'what is this, some kind of interrogation?'

Tina ignored him. I busied myself for a second, loading the
shredded lettuce into a Tupperware bowl. Another helper put
two sagging loaves of sliced white bread beside it. A thick,

sugary smell drifted from the stove, where store-donated cans of franks and beans had been emptied into a big saucepan.

'My father's in Vermont,' I told Tina. 'He has a sister here in the city.'

Selwyn turned away with a shrug.

Tina went on: 'Sister, huh? She have children?'

'She has two sons.'

'Your cousins.'

'That's right—'

'You been married?'

'No, I've never been married. What about you?'

'You a homo?'

'No, I'm not, as a matter of fact.'

'Girlfriend, right?'

'Not at the moment. Shall we help them set the table?'

'She leave you for some other guy?'

'No—'

'You leave her?'

'I suppose so, yes.'

Tina grinned. 'Uh-huh. Uh-huh. I got a favour I might have to ask you, Simon.'

'Please do. I'd be very glad to help.'

'You a lawyer, right?'

'No, I'm afraid I'm not a lawyer.'

'Oh. But you a Jew?'

'Yes, why? What did you want to ask?'

Her eyes slid away, then settled again on mine. They were delicately curved at the outer corners, thin little oases in the otherwise harsh landscape of her face. She broke into a whispery laugh.

'I'm jiving you, man. I'm jiving you.'

She put her hand on my wrist. The hand felt light and hard as a bird's foot. She went on with her questioning. After it ended a strained feeling lingered with me, as if I had been exposed to something more turbulent and oppressive than had appeared to be the case.

At dinner on my third week since Tina's appearance, I saw that people no longer attempted to bring her into the conversation. Subalowsky, demonstrating how he had got the repetitive motion injury that had paralysed his hand (he had been a barman, and he mimed a drink-pouring action with his stiffened, fin-like limb), managed a curious rift or lacuna in the arc of his gaze that succeeded in excluding Tina entirely as he looked around the table, drawing in his tribute of laughter. She sat in her own dark sphere, small and isolated. I thought I could see in her expression something of a shunned child's defiant pride in proving to itself a kind of negative mastery of circumstances. In a professional way I felt concerned for her. But I had not taken to her personally, and my sympathies were with the other residents, whom I knew to be unusually tolerant of the foibles and weaknesses of their fellow humans.

That night, as I came out of the volunteers' bathroom at the top of the ramp that led up from the annexe to the sacristy entrance of the church, I heard a sound to the right of me, from inside the church. Looking through the doorway, I saw Tina standing next to a pillar, lit by the dim glow of the sconce lamps that hung over the main entrance. She was wearing a bathrobe of brown towelling. Her feet and legs were bare.

'Hi,' she whispered.

'Hello, Tina.'

'How you doing?'

'I'm fine, thank you. How are you?'

'All right.'

I waited, still standing by the bathroom door, several paces from her. Except in emergencies, this part of the building was strictly off limits to residents, and by my distance, as well as by a deliberate sternness in my manner, I was intending to convey the suggestion of a rebuke on behalf of the shelter, without going so far as to say anything direct.

'Was there something you wanted?'

She grinned, putting a finger over her lips. Then, beckoning me to follow, she stepped away from the pillar, farther back into the shadows of the church. Uneasy, but reluctant to assert myself any more forcefully at this moment, I followed her into one of the wooden pews. She slid along to the far end, patting the space beside her. I sat where she had motioned. We were in near-darkness here, the surroundings visible only as pale strokes of light over prominences or the uneven parts of polished surfaces—stone wings, the angled lip of the pulpit. Two parallel gleams like dim copper showed in Tina's lap where her thin thighs came out of the bathrobe. The same stale, dry scent of sandalwood that I had caught before was upon her. As a purely physical sensation I was aware of her flimsiness, her physical vulnerability and near-nakedness beside me. I felt the awkwardness of my position and sensed that I should not have allowed myself to be led here. Possibly, it occurred to me, there was an element of gratuitous manipulation on Tina's part, a simple revelling in being able to make the volunteer do what she asked. As I thought back to our conversation the previous week, the mention of a favour, it crossed my mind also that she had come here to beg or perhaps beguile a sum of money from me. I looked up at the ceiling, bracing myself for a difficult conversation.

Beside me on the pew there was movement: an arm rising, a whisper of clothing. I became aware of Tina's hand sliding under the lapel of her robe as if to withdraw something.

'Look,' I heard.

Her hand was at the lapel, cupped tightly as if she were half afraid to reveal its contents. It took me several seconds to realise that what she was showing me was in fact a thickly folded wad of bills.

'Two hundred seventy dollars.' She held it out towards me. 'You take it.' It seemed she was urging the small bundle onto me. 'You hold it for me, okay?' I said nothing, not fully comprehending. She spoke again, in a hoarse whisper: 'You look after it for me, right? I'm not legal in this country. I can't get a bank. You be my banker.'

She found my hand in the darkness and pressed the money into it.

In my private embarrassment at my earlier conjecture, my grateful surprise at having had it proved wrong, I heard myself agreeing with alacrity to do what she asked. I wasn't even able to bring myself to count the money in her presence.

I counted it under the bedside lamp in the volunteers' annexe and saw that it was as she had said: two hundred and seventy dollars. The bills were very soft and frail, the print worn off in places from repeated foldings. They were warm too, and gave off a fragrance of sandalwood.

In the morning I handed Tina a receipt for the money, with my telephone number on the back of the piece of paper. In case she needed cash during the week, I put the money—the bills themselves—into a desk drawer at my apartment.

It grew there, a little larger every week. Tina didn't offer to tell me where it came from, and in keeping with the tacit code of conduct for volunteers, I didn't ask. It would have been difficult to imagine a legitimate source.

The bright air of late autumn dissolved into blustery rain and sleet. The city, almost South American in summer, shed the last of its carnival colour and turned into a chilly European metropolis: grey, wet, and miserable. Darkness poured into the day at both ends. Under the projects the leafless pin-oaks and ailanthus trees caught their winter foliage of tattered plastic bags.

In fairness to myself I should say that I realised almost immediately that I had made a mistake in allowing myself to become involved in Tina's affairs. Quite apart from the fact that the shelter organisers would almost certainly not have approved of one of their members acting as private banker for a resident, it soon became apparent to me that the arrangement was having little or no stabilising effect on Tina's behaviour at the shelter. She continued to be unsociable, if not downright aggressive, and this made me nervous about my position.

By the time the pile of bills in my desk drawer had risen to almost five hundred dollars, I was beginning to think that I should disengage myself. One night I made an attempt to do so.

We were at the top of the ramp, by the sacristy entrance to the church, where Tina had come, as usual, to give me the week's installment. I put it to her that she might feel safer keeping her money with the shelter organisers than with me. I said I was sure the coordinator would be willing to make a similar arrangement, and that there would be no danger of him reporting her to the Immigration authorities.

'What's the matter,' Tina said immediately, 'you don't want to help me no more?'

'No, I just had a feeling you might not be happy with the way things stood at the moment.'

An expression that was both wounded and suspicious came into her face.

'You don't want to help me no more.'

'Of course I want to help you, Tina.'

'No, man, you don't want to help me.'

She stood in a stiff, angular pose, breathing deeply through her nostrils, as if absorbed in sombre and disturbing reflection. Her hand was still at the lapel of her bathrobe, where it had gone in anticipation of giving me the money.

'What can I say, Tina? I want to help you very much.'

'You saying you don't want to help me. That's what I'm hearing.'

Her voice was rising. I felt trapped and agitated, sensing a convergence of ancient, unknowable sorrows with a possible talent for histrionics. I wondered too whether I was perhaps after all being too scrupulously cautious. In my own conscience I already stood accused of lacking genuine sympathy for her, and it struck me now that I might also be guilty of setting my own peace of mind above hers, in a way that was both cowardly and unnecessary.

'I was only making a suggestion,' I heard myself say in a yielding voice.

She looked at me with her lips tightly closed. I felt unable to press the point any further.

'Why don't you give me the money and we'll forget I said anything?'

I held out my hand for the money. But with her instinct for the psychological advantage, she tightened the towelling robe at her neck instead of giving me the money and stepped back. She stared at me, saying nothing. A bright moistness showed under the soft bluish lashes of her eyes. I looked back at her, unsure what to say or do.

'Why don't you give it to me?' I said gently.

Again she tugged at the lapel of the towelling robe, leaving her forearm across her breast with a protective air. The soles of her feet showed light and yellowish under her heels.

'You don't like me.'

'I do like you, Tina.'

'No, man, I don't think you like me.'

I put my hand appeasingly on her arm.

'Come on, Tina, I like you very much.'

'Why you don't want to help me, then?'

She stood stiffly, looking obstinately away from me. For a moment something quite acutely touching and poignant seemed expressed in the posture. I squeezed her arm lightly with my hand. She softened in my grip. Looking into my eyes, she took a step forward. As she did, I felt an unexpected stirring: almost as much in response, I think, to a sudden glimpse of her reality as a human being, unobscured by the veil of ideas and surmises which in my ignorance I had woven around her, as to the sense of her reality as a woman. I drew back, surprised at myself. Her eyes flickered over me. She looked pretty and knowing.

'Come on, now,' I said, reverting to my brisker manner, 'let me take the money and we'll go on with things the way they were.'

She drew the limp, dust-grey and green bundle from the inside pocket of her robe and held it close to her.

I put my hand out to take it, but she continued to hold it back.

'Give it to me, Tina. I'll look after it.'

Still, she didn't offer the little bundle. An almost playful look of contrariness came into her face, as if on an inexplicable whim she had now decided to tease me with the money. Exasperated, both with her and with myself for handling the situation so badly, I spoke impatiently.

'Give me the money, Tina!'

It came out more harshly than I had intended, but the effect was swift. She gave me a peculiar smile, at once submissive and satisfied.

'Okay, Simon'—she spoke in a tone that I can only describe as coquettish—'you the boss.'

She handed me the money and walked away with light, quick steps. I stood for a while, uncertain what had passed between us, sensing that I had in some way been appropriated into the fantastical afflictions of a soul more disturbed than I had yet realised, and that far from bringing our arrangement to an end, I had become more deeply implicated in it than before.

In December I spent a week at my father's farmhouse in Vermont. His wife's two daughters were there with their husbands and children. Four feet of snow lay on the ground outside. In the afternoons we went up into the sparkling woods on cross-country skis, watching the landscape unfold beneath us as we climbed: frozen ponds and diamond-bright meadows, church spires whittled sharp as the icicles dangling from the shingles of the gold-windowed Capes and cabins. Leafless maples rolled like cannon smoke through the dark evergreens. At night, after the children had been put to bed, we sat in the resplendent glow of the glass-doored stove in the living-room, talking and drinking, gazing out through the windows at the white birches standing luminously against the shadowy volumes of my father's barn: an enormous, bulging building, stocked like an ark with two or more of everything—two cars, two pickup trucks, two deep freezes, two canoes, skis two by two in racks along the walls . . .

I arrived back in New York on the day I was due at the shelter and went straight there from Penn Station.

There were lilies in the crypt and a jug of yellow chrysanthemums on the refectory table.

I had never seen flowers at the shelter before, and the sight startled me.

Looking about, I noticed that the place had been given a thorough cleaning. The soot on the globe lamps had been wiped off, and the opaque glass sparkled overhead. All the zinc surfaces were gleaming. A clean, pleasant smell of furniture polish filled the TV room.

In the volunteers' annexe I opened the cupboard where emergency numbers and occasional messages were left. There was a note inside: *To those of you I haven't yet reached: Tina D'Oliveira arrived two nights running under obvious influence of narcotics, and we had to ask her to leave. This is very distressing for us all, but you'll appreciate we're obliged to enforce our few rules strictly. In Tina's place we have a newcomer, Geraldine Leal, who as you will see has already made her*

117

*presence felt in the shelter. As ever, please do all you can to make her feel welcome at St. Ursula's.* The note was signed by Abel McCormick, the coordinator of the program.

I closed the cupboard door and went back into the kitchen to put on coffee for the residents. I remember standing at the shiny zinc counter, spooning coffee grounds into the big frilled filter. The chrysanthemums on the table were a brighter yellow than the kitchen's low-wattage bulbs, giving their tangled heads an overbrimming, incandescent appearance that fused itself into the still not fully absorbed impact of what I had read, and seemed at that moment the vehicle of imminent catastrophe pressing through from the hypothetical into the real. I reminded myself that I had given Tina my telephone number, and this gave me a feeling of at least provisional calm.

At dinner I asked what had happened.

'They throwed her out,' the woman called Lucky said with a shrug.

Subalowsky described it: 'She showed up Sunday night barely able to stand on her two feet. The volunteer said he couldn't let her into the shelter in that condition. He told her to straighten out before she came back. Next night she comes back even worse. Jessica was the volunteer that night. She told Tina she couldn't come in, but she wouldn't leave. She pulled out a Sheetrock knife and stood in the doorway yelling and screaming, threatening anyone who came near her . . .'

Selwyn broke in: 'She spit at me! She spit at me!'

'Jessica had to telephone Mr McCormick. He came over right away. Told Tina she was out of the program and to take her things and leave right away or he'd call the cops.'

'And she left?'

'Yep. She left.'

There were no expressions of sympathy, and the conversation soon turned to lighter matters. I had the impression that the residents were satisfied, not just with the removal of an unstable element from their midst, but with the severity of the shelter's rules; that they took a stern pleasure in seeing them enforced.

After dinner I went straight to the volunteers' annexe and sat on the hard plastic chair. Contented murmurs reached me from the crypt. The heating knocked in the pipes and hissed with a long, bubbling suspiration. I thought of the money in my desk drawer at home and told myself again that I had given Tina my telephone number; that even if she had lost it, she could get hold of me through the shelter.

But with the image of the soft, sweet-smelling pile of bills nestling among my papers came a feeling of oppressive disclosure, as if I were being presented with a sudden privileged inward glimpse into my position at the shelter. In what was still effectively the shock of the moment, the circumstances seemed to me to embody more than they could perhaps be said to contain on the basis of a rational analysis. As I write now I think of Frantz Fanon's austere stipulation. "It is necessary at all times and in all places to make explicit, to demystify, and to harry the insult to mankind that exists in oneself." Precisely that passive, unintended, but nevertheless culpable relation was what seemed exposed in me, and no doubt what this connection lacked in logic was more than made up for by my abundant willingness to take a symbolic or even superstitious interpretation of anything pertaining to my own uneasy status as volunteer. What was a volunteer, someone who wanted to help or someone who wanted to guard the door? Were our motives ones of simple charity, or did we suffer from some morbid wish to enact within our own psyches, to illuminate by our own lives, the essential relations between one part of society and another, just as the sin-eaters of another century elected to absorb into themselves both the wrongs and the due punishment of their sinning brethren? It was like being shown an X-ray of some part of your body, your chest, for

instance, the physician pointing to a bright, calcined macula-
tion behind the ribs: a surprise, certainly, but one that nevertheless seems to confirm something you had always known
without knowing that you knew it.

The next day I made inquiries with the police and at other
shelters in the city: nobody had heard of Tina. At that point
I told Abel McCormick what had happened. He apparently
thought it unnecessary to reprimand me for allowing myself
to get into such a situation, and instead merely suggested that
I hand over Tina's money to the shelter, on the understanding
that it would be given back to her if she turned up to claim
it. I wrote out a cheque at once and used the cash she had
given me for my own expenses. The smell of sandalwood
lingered in my desk, and long after I had spent the last of the
bills, the sweet, dry fragrance would rise up from the folds of
my wallet whenever I opened it to make a purchase.

Two or three weeks passed without a word from Tina.
Whether she ever turned up at the shelter after that to claim
her money I have no idea. In February I began a new job and
I no longer had time to work as a volunteer.

I did, however, see Tina on one more occasion.

I had turned into a quiet, dilapidated block just south of
Houston, on my way to have dinner with a friend on the
Lower East Side. Light, sharp sleet was falling, briefly flu-
orescent where it slanted down through the red-and-gold il-
luminations of a store on the corner. Granular residue shone
on broken stones where the sidewalk had erupted under pressure of tree roots or burst water pipes. Fire escapes clung to
the fronts of the tenements on my side of the street, saggy and
rusty, with a ponderous ornateness like the weavings of a bat-
talion of cast-iron spiders. Most of the opposite side was empty
lots—boarded up or fenced off with padlocked chain link and
looped razor-wire.

On that side, near the far end of the block, a figure had emerged from a gap between two sheets of corrugated iron and set off swiftly in my direction. As we came closer to each other I saw that it was Tina. A feeling of relief surged in me, though it became rapidly tinged with apprehension as she approached.

She was walking at a fierce pace. Her hands were working at her sides, and she seemed to be expostulating as she moved. She hadn't noticed me, or at least hadn't seen that it was me. I looked at her as she came nearer. The jerkiness in her walk was more pronounced than I had seen it before—a suggestion of involuntary movement flickering over each footstep. The impression was of some hostile emotion metabolised into the actual musculature; echoed strangely, like a kind of livid afterglow, by the indecipherable but peculiarly expressive graffiti on the boards she passed, the word-forms midway along an apparent regression from alphabetic to hieroglyphic: some spattered out, some creamed out in a bendy, lubricious strut, others glowering in a hallucinatory rainbow smoulder; all of them suggestive of some dense extrusion of human fury and wonder. A rapid, unintelligible mutter became audible: imprecations, by the look on her face. Either side of her, her stiffened, spread-out fingers were jabbing at the air. She looked packed tight with violence, like a bristling mine ready to explode at the slightest touch. As we came level, I saw from a rolling whiteness in her eyes that she was probably not in a condition to recognise me.

'Tina!' I called out.

She plunged on past me. I crossed over, feeling a lightness in my limbs as I ran after her.

'Tina,' I said, catching up with her. She strode on, fast and oblivious, her muttered words no more distinct at this proximity than from across the street. I reached out with my hand.

'Tina, it's me, Simon.' I touched her on the shoulder.

She spun around. A look of terror shone in her narrow eyes,

which seemed not to see me so much as to search for me through an enveloping veil of darkness, one of her hands appearing partly to grope, partly to pummel at the space between us. I reached into my coat, intending at the very least to make her take whatever I had in my wallet. As I pulled it out, I felt what seemed like the whiplash of a white hot wire across my knuckles; a sensation that left me stupefied for a moment, with nothing in my mind except Subalowsky's phrase *Sheetrock knife,* flashing there like a message on a console in an empty office. I stood there with my hand spread before me, a string of blood-beads swelling across the shallow cut, the smell of sandalwood hanging in the air—fragrance of a desolation beyond the reach of pity or even understanding; of a reproach too deep and bitter for forgiveness—while Tina sped off with the same peculiar stammering articulation, as if in the painful embrace of some invisible, ratcheting, mechanical apparatus, the big, glittering coils of razor wire running along the wooden boards above her like a new and savage decorative order.

# Three Evenings

1

Jonathan was twenty-two when he met Katie Vairish, and he was new to London. Katie was older than him by six years. A cousin of Jonathan's introduced them at a wedding reception in Surrey, where Jonathan had grown up and several of his relatives lived. The cousin described him as an aspiring journalist, and the ghost of a smile crossed Katie Vairish's face.

She wore high heels and a sleeveless crushed-velvet dress with fingerprint-like smudges gleaming all over it in the electric light. Her brown hair was cut in a short bob, leaving the smooth curves of her neck and shoulders bare except for a thin necklace of coral and silver. Her name sounded familiar to Jonathan; vaguely, and for some reason also a little forbiddingly. She made him nervous, but whether out of capriciousness or because his diffident manner genuinely endeared him to her, she seemed to make up her mind to like him. Before they parted she wrote down his number and promised to commission something from him for the magazine where she worked as an editor.

He had finished university six months before, with a degree in history, and the offer of a place to do postgraduate work, which he had declined. To the extent that he believed a moment would arrive in his life when he would be the author of a number of written works, his cousin's description of him was not wholly inaccurate. What these works would be about he had no idea, but this didn't trouble him.

He was dark, and of slight build. His eyes were brown, but the pigment was thinly concentrated in the vane of the irises, giving them a translucent look that was the most striking aspect of his appearance.

Otherwise there was an indistinctness about him: he was like something that had not quite set. He was aware of this, but it didn't trouble him any more than the content of his unwritten books did. He believed what he had read in Kierkegaard about the self: that its task 'is to become itself'; and he felt that he had a long time to accomplish this task. At a certain point his nature would declare itself more forcefully and he would step forward to take his place in the world. How he occupied himself in the meantime was unimportant. It didn't matter to him that the walls of the room he rented in Acton were streaked yellow with damp, that the furniture was hideous, the curtains and carpets embedded with the dirt of his predecessors. Nor did it matter much to him what he did for money: he interrogated train passengers for a market-research company; he taught history 'O' and 'A' level at a crammer in Holborn. All of this was temporary and unimportant to him; he was just camping down in his life for the time being.

Over a period of two years Katie commissioned perhaps a dozen pieces from him—trivial things mostly: reviews of consumer exhibitions at Olympia, interviews with up-and-coming actors or chefs. It amused him to write them, though after a while he took the work less because he needed it than for the excuse to visit Katie in her office high over the Euston Road.

Unlike as they were—she with her trailing aura of gossipy dinner parties, her six years' seniority; he with his taciturn and slightly provincial air—a subdued but nevertheless suspenseful interest in one another had grown up between them. And although the intervals between his visits were long, each one brought about a perceptible deepening of this interest.

She was pretty in a languid, rather overdelicate way, with big, long-lashed eyes, high cheekbones, and bluish skin. She was very thin, a heavy smoker, always well-dressed in furling outfits of black or grey, with a rosebud or a brooch or a hand-pleated silk scarf for colour.

In the soft leather chairs of her office, with the blinds half-closed against the evening sky and the rush-hour traffic crawling like two metal-scaled serpents in the dusk below, they would drink gin and tonics and talk together with a warm and effortless intimacy. It was perhaps this quality, this effortlessness, that Jonathan valued most about their friendship. He felt relaxed with Katie and under no pressure to disclose what wasn't yet ready for disclosure. Other women tended to take his quietness as a ploy to keep them at arm's length, or else as the sign of a superior wisdom, which usually resulted in disappointment, when in fact it was just that he was still more or less a mystery to himself. Katie, on the other hand, with the simple egotism of an attractive woman unused to probing her own inclinations, merely adapted his quietness to her own needs: she made him the repository of her confidences, and this suited him. He was a good listener, and many of their conversations consisted of little more than Katie complaining about the men—the barristers, merchant bankers, or television producers—that she got herself involved with, while Jonathan murmured sympathetically in response.

At the same time, with a characteristic disregard for apparent inconsistency that lent her life a curious plasticity, she flirted with Jonathan when the mood took her, and it was settled between them that they were attracted to each other; a fact that gave their discussions of her lovers an undercurrent of faint tragedy.

When they parted company for the night, Katie would say goodbye in a way that made it seem as if their separation was simply an inconvenience, a quirk of fate that had to be put up with for the time being but would eventually be corrected. She would put her mouth to his, and on one occasion she opened her lips a little, without actually opening her mouth, but staying like that for a moment, looking up at him intently from under her long lashes before pulling away. He happened to be involved at that time with a woman at the tutorial college where he taught, a fact which Katie knew perfectly well. He went home feeling exhilarated and bewildered, the after-impression of her lips lingering in a sweet taste of perfume and cigarette smoke.

Sometimes they would go out together for a drink or a meal. Once, about a year and a half into their acquaintance, when Katie had moved into a new flat, they went to an auction in Fulham. Jonathan hadn't been to an auction before.

'You've never been to an auction? Oh, they're the most exciting things. It's like going to the races, only being the jockey as well as the person betting.'

The auction house was in a quiet street between an office building and a row of antique shops with their shutters down. It looked as if it had once been a warehouse: sombre Victorian brick on the outside, chilly and cavernous inside, with bare floorboards and dusty white globe lamps hanging on chains from iron beams.

There was a pulpit, a real pulpit, for the auctioneer. Rows of chairs stood in front of it, waiting for the prospective buyers to settle. Around these, and spreading back through several more rooms, pieces of furniture and cabinets of bric-a-brac were heaped densely together, stark-looking and mysteriously drained of colour by the glare of the white lamps.

Dozens of people, most of them smartly dressed and in

couples, milled about the cluttered rooms examining table-
legs and sofa-backs, looking for hallmarks on cutlery, pressing
the keys of upright pianos, checking tea-sets for cracks and
Oriental rugs for stains. Amused, slightly sheepish expressions
were visible on many faces, as if their owners were unsure of
the dignity of the ceremony, or at least felt it necessary to build
up a playfully ironic attitude towards the imminent public
declarations of taste and acquisitive will. There was a slight
tense gaiety in the air, as at the beginning of a social function.
Against the orphaned clutter, with its faint aura of misfortune,
the human beings looked bright and predatory.

Katie and Jonathan wandered about, looking at the estimates
in the stapled catalogue they had picked up from the entrance
and marking off items that appealed to Katie—a mirror with
a pear-wood frame, a sloping school desk with an inkwell,
woollen fruits under a glass dome.

'This is fun, isn't it, Jonathan?'

Jonathan smiled at her, catching the look of anticipated
pleasure in her eyes.

She was carrying her coat and wearing a short dress with
the flowery black lace tights that were fashionable that year.
Her lithe figure drew glances from the men who passed her.
Normally a little pallid, her face took on a delicate glow against
the inanimate background. Against these things she had the
pale, slightly improbably incandescence of a winter flower
against snow. Her scent rose, now and then, lightly over the
dull must of wood and iron. Looking at her Jonathan felt a
momentary, curious anguish, and a wish to deny to himself
that he thought her beautiful. He wondered if people could
tell that he and she were not a couple furnishing their home
together. He thought that they probably could, and he tried
to work out why this should be so. Without forming any very
definite conclusions, he found the thought converging unexpectedly with his sense of the effortlessness of their relations

with each other, and the idea that these two things might be connected disturbed him so much that he immediately turned his attention to something else.

They came to a partitioned room that appeared to be devoted to lighting fixtures. There were upright lamps, table lamps, wall sconces, track lights, lampshades of every description. At the far end were chandeliers, hanging from a bar or sitting on the bare floor. Most of these chandeliers were glass, with cobwebby riggings and thick coats of dust over their faceted lustres, but on the floor in the corner was a more resplendent-looking one, made entirely of gilded ironwork. A man in a camel-hair coat was bending over it, fingering the matt gold radial of looping bulb-holders. Clusters of oak leaves and acorns sprouted all over the armature, very delicately moulded in the same gilt iron; the leaves almost leaf-thin, wobbling a little in the light as the man examined them with a thick finger and thumb.

Katie paused to look at it from the doorway.

'God, isn't that lovely?'

She went over to the corner, moving in deft steps and turns like a graceful forest animal through a small grove of standard lamps, and leant down to touch the chandelier. Jonathan followed behind.

'Don't you think it's rather wonderful, Jonathan?'

'Quite nice,' Jonathan said.

'I mean, it's nothing special, but it's cheerful, and I could do with a few cheerful things . . .'

The man who had been examining the chandelier stood up. Katie smiled at him vaguely. He looked away and moved on, marking his sheet.

'Yes, I think I might bid for that,' Katie said. 'Do you see what the estimate is?'

Jonathan looked through the catalogue.

'Sixty-five pounds.'

'Well. I should think it'll go for double that. They usually give a low estimate, to make you start thinking of it as your own. But that's all right; it's worth double, wouldn't you say?'

'If you can afford it.'

'I think so. I'm quite taken with it. I think I could go up to a hundred and thirty for it.' She turned to Jonathan; a lively look had come into her eyes.

He smiled at her.

'No higher, though,' she said. 'You have to make up your mind in advance, otherwise you get carried away. Stop me at a hundred and thirty, would you?'

'All right.'

'I mean it. Shut me up at a hundred and thirty if the bidding's still going.'

'If you say so.'

'I do say so.'

Soon after that a bell rang and people took their seats for the auction.

A young man with a bow tie and a yellow silk handkerchief mounted the pulpit. Porters in green boiler-suits collected below him, and a bespectacled woman sat at a table with a ledger. A big reflector heater was switched on and the two thick bars glowed brightly in their wire cage, sending out a wave of raw heat into the chilly room.

After winking and mouthing hellos at various members of his congregation, the auctioneer banged his gavel and went over the rules of the auction.

'Signal clearly, I can't read your thoughts. Those of you with epilepsy or St Vitus Dance kindly sit on your hands unless you wish to leave here with a large amount of unwanted possessions. All successful bids are final and binding. A porter will take your name between lots and I will personally have you gently poached in fish broth if you try telling Phyllis here that you've changed your mind . . .'

There was a little laughter. Katie leaned in close to Jonathan, smiling. The auction began.

It was fast and efficient. Moveable lots were brought rapidly across the front by the porters. The heavier items were described by the auctioneer, always with a little self-important glimmer of facetiousness. There were more than two hundred lots, and after a while a mesmerising rhythm set in.

Four or five pieces that Katie had marked were sold off in bursts of bidding that she took part in briefly, with a short, excited flare like dry tinder being swept over by a grass fire, clutching Jonathan's arm with her free hand while she bid and letting it go when her limit was passed.

She hadn't bought anything by the time the light fixtures took their turn in the procession of objects passing beneath the pulpit. Jonathan could sense a keener attention stirring in her as they appeared. He himself felt more alert and invigorated, following as always when he was with her the fluctuations of her mood.

Lamps went by in quick succession, seeming by the steadiness of movement more to metamorphose into one another than give way to each other. There was a stream of glass shades with frosting and floral ornamentation. Then the chandeliers began, slung on poles between porters like strange shot-down creatures of the upper air, their dusty glass plumage hanging limp. Katie sat forward on her seat, her back very straight, her lips pursed in concentration. In one hand she held the catalogue, rolled up like a baton. With the other, as her chandelier made its entrance from the wings, she grasped Jonathan's arm.

The bidding started at twenty pounds and rose rapidly, with bids from all over the room. After sixty-five pounds—the catalogue estimate—the pace slowed a little. The seven or eight people bidding dropped to four, and at eighty-five pounds there appeared to be only two other people apart from Katie. Looking around, Jonathan saw an elderly woman, who had already bought a number of things in a rather professional, detached manner, nod when ninety pounds was asked for. Katie raised her rolled-up catalogue at ninety-five, and a figure—the man in the camel-hair coat whom they had seen examining the chandelier earlier—turned round from two rows ahead of them, catching sight of Katie's signal before turning back and nodding at a hundred pounds.

'One hundred pounds. One hundred pounds.' The auctioneer said, 'I'm bid one hundred pounds. Who'll give me one hundred and five? Yes madam. Yes other madam one hundred and ten . . .'

The chandelier hung in the reddish light from the electric heater, looking bright and festive with its delicate sprays of oak leaves and acorns.

'One hundred and ten pounds. Am I bid one hundred and fifteen?'

The auctioneer looked at the elderly woman, who gave a dry little shake of her head.

'One hundred and ten pounds, then.'

Jonathan prepared himself now, like an actor with a small part girding himself up for his entrance. He sensed that Katie had given him this role as a way of making him feel he was wanted, and he appreciated the gesture; the more so because of the uncharacteristic thoughtfulness it conveyed.

The man in the camel-hair coat nodded.

'Yes. One hundred and fifteen.'

Katie raised her catalogue. Her other hand had tightened on Jonathan's arm, and he could feel her excitement in the grip.

'One hundred and twenty. One hundred and twenty-five. This is a superb piece as you can see. Comes from a most distinguished home. Knew its father and mother myself . . .'

Light laughter escaped briefly from the hush of the room.

'One hundred and twenty-five pounds.'

Jonathan whispered to Katie, 'Remember, this is your limit.'
She raised her catalogue.

'Yes, one hundred and thirty pounds.'

The man immediately bid.

'One hundred and thirty-five pounds.'

Jonathan tapped the hand that was holding his arm.

'Stop now.'

Katie frowned briefly without turning to him and raised her catalogue.

'Yes, madam, one hundred and forty pounds. I'm bid one hundred and forty pounds . . .'

Jonathan wasn't sure what to do. He had not anticipated resistance, and now he was unsure of the seriousness of Katie's request. The man in front nodded and Katie at once raised her catalogue. Her eyes were wide open, and there was a look of taut, gleeful determination on her face.

'Yes, sir. One hundred and fifty-five pounds. Still a bargain at that *if* I may say so. A charming piece, one hundred and sixty pounds, yes. One hundred and sixty pounds.'

What should he do? The situation seemed to rebuke him for lacking force. He took hold of Katie's shoulder and shook it firmly. 'You're over your limit,' he whispered, trying to sound good-humoured.

The man in front nodded and glanced round. He was short, but very broad across the shoulders, with a fleshy, pugnacious face and thick ginger eyebrows. Jonathan squeezed Katie's shoulder again as she raised her catalogue.

'Katie,' he whispered sternly. 'Katie, stop now.'

'Oh, be quiet.' She wriggled free of his grasp and gave him an angry look. He sat back, feeling as if he had been slapped.

'Am I bid one hundred and seventy-five pounds? Magnificent piece of craftsmanship. Former ear-ring off a giantess, no. Yes. One hundred and seventy-five pounds. One hundred and eighty. One eighty-five. One ninety. One hundred and ninety pounds. I'm bid one hundred and ninety pounds.'

Jonathan looked at Katie. Her face was flushed, her eyes were bright with an intent, malevolent look of pleasure in them. She had never spoken to him in that way before, and he didn't know how he should react. He felt taunted and in a dim way responsible for it himself.

The man in the camel-hair coat bid a hundred and ninety-five pounds. Katie at once signalled two hundred.

'Two hundred pounds,' the auctioneer crowed, pursing his lips in a way that seemed to suggest he was sharing a joke with certain select members of the audience. 'I'm bid two hundred pounds. We rise now in increments of ten pounds. Am I bid two hundred and ten pounds. Two hundred and ten?' He looked at the man in the camel-hair coat, raising his eyebrows. There was no signal.

'Two hundred pounds it is, then. For two hundred pounds this, ah, illuminating creation, going, going, gone!' He banged his gavel and proceeded to the next lot.

After the auction was over Katie paid the cashier, and they made their way out of the building. Jonathan carried the chandelier, which was heavy and awkward to hold without bending the sprigs of oak leaves and acorns. His feeling of injury had not disappeared; if anything, it seemed to be growing stronger.

'You didn't do a very good job of keeping me under control, did you?' Katie said with a smile.

'What was I supposed to do? Tie you up and gag you?'

Katie shrugged, declining to acknowledge the petulant note in his voice.

As they left the building they caught up with the man who had bid against Katie for the chandelier. He had lit a small cigar, and the whole of his stocky, corpulent frame seemed absorbed in smoking it. Night had fallen and it was cold outside. Katie put on the short suede coat that she had been carrying and gave a little shiver. She turned as she passed the man.

'I hope you didn't have your heart set on it—' She tilted her head at the chandelier in Jonathan's hands. A grin with a distant look of insolence in it turned up the corners of her lips. The man stopped and looked at her, drawing on his cigar. Under his coat he wore a grey suit and a pinstripe shirt with a white collar that seemed too tight for his thick neck. Starched cuffs with mother-of-pearl cuff links showed at his wrists. There was a glowering and dissipated look about him, a heavy metropolitan ripeness of early middle age. Removing the cigar from his mouth, he gave a dry look.

'I'll survive,' he said.

Katie eyed him with an abstracted expression for a moment. Jonathan hung beside her, holding the heavy chandelier. People jostled past them along the lamplit street, many with satisfied looks, their arms full of plunder.

'I've just moved into a new flat,' Katie said. 'I hadn't thought of getting a chandelier. I think the glass ones are fairly vile. But when I saw this I thought it would go rather well.'

The man considered this, glancing briefly at Jonathan and turning back to Katie. Jonathan shifted the weight of the chandelier, pointedly, but Katie did not appear to notice.

'Well, there you are,' the man said, and gave a little nod. 'It's yours now.'

'You don't feel deprived, then?'

'I expect if I'd wanted it badly enough I'd have got it.' He made to go. Jonathan looked at the loose, heavy flesh of his face, willing him away.

'I bet it was a present for someone,' Katie called out.

The man turned. 'As a matter of fact,' he said, then gave a thin, superior smile of his own, 'as a matter of fact, that's none of your business.'

Katie laughed. 'Well, don't worry, there's always something here. I come just about every week at the moment. I usually find something I like.'

A flush of dismay went through Jonathan. His arms ached from the heaviness of the chandelier, and the unpleasantness of the situation seemed to add to its weight.

The man nodded again and marched off. Jonathan watched his squat figure disappear down the lamplit street. He turned to Katie, who gave him a distracted smile and looked about for a taxi.

At home he lay on his bed, going over the evening in his mind.

He thought again of how Katie had asked him to stop her from overbidding, and how he had failed to do so. Well, he could hardly blame himself for that. He had no authority over Katie, and there was nothing in their relationship that gave him any claim on her obedience, even as an instrument of her own will. The sensible reaction would be to shrug off the incident as a case of perversity on Katie's part that perhaps didn't reflect well on her but said nothing about himself.

But the incident had lodged itself in him with an oppressive weight, and he was unable to shrug it off. It seemed to accuse him of a weakness that went deeper and deeper the more he considered it. He saw that either he should not have allowed himself to get into such a position in the first place, or having done so, he should have been effectual. On what basis, by what actions, he could have asserted the necessary authority he did not know, but he sensed that it could have been done and that another man might have managed it in his place.

He thought of the casually imperious way in which Katie had shut him up, and a feeling of bitterness welled in him. It struck him that he should have walked out there and then. Anyone with an ounce of pride would have done just that. He pictured himself doing so and, finding in the image a certain satisfaction, pictured it again, and then again. But at the time it hadn't even occurred to him! And not only had he stayed,

but he had also meekly carried the chandelier out of the auction house like a lackey; or no, like a prisoner forced to parade
in public carrying the instrument of his own torture . . . And
as if that wasn't enough, having allowed himself to be insulted
and used as a convenient pair of arms, he had then stood by
uncomplainingly while Katie had obliquely but unmistakably
made an assignation with another man!

He thought of his own lyrical, tender, patient desire for
Katie; of how with minimum effort she kept its ardent little
flame alight, and of how he had contentedly accepted that this
should be so. It came to him that he disliked her. At the same
time he felt a harsh and narrow craving for her.

He got up and closed the heavy curtains. He undressed and
went to the basin in the corner of the room. In the mirror
over the basin he saw his face, and what he saw did not please
him. The pale, translucent eyes that Katie herself had once
told him were beautiful seemed to him unbearably soft and
beseeching. He poured a glass of water and lay back down on
the bed.

Gradually his feeling of dissatisfaction spread from Katie
into matters that had nothing to do with her. He saw that he
was the same withheld, closed-up individual that he had been
when he left university almost two years before. But whereas
then he had been confident of the presence of all sorts of
splendours preparing themselves inside him, he now found
himself wondering if there was anything of interest there at
all.

He thought of his unworldliness, and for the first time suspected it of being no more than a kind of congealed imma-
turity. And his days coaching the 'O'- and 'A'-level failures
or walking up and down the corridors of trains; the nights in
the bed between the wardrobe with its cracked veneer and the
gold rivulets of damp coursing down the floral wallpaper; were
these situations perhaps slyly taking advantage of his dreamy

passivity to exchange their transitory status in his life for one of permanence? A mortified feeling came into him. He turned off the table lamp. The gas fire was on and he left it to burn up the fifty pence he had put in the meter. Under watery-blue flames the clay glowed bright pink and orange, throwing crimson shadows into the dark room.

Not long after this, Jonathan decided that it would be a good thing for him if he went and lived abroad for a period.

His natural inertia, as well as an exaggerated idea of the difficulty of earning a living in a foreign country, kept him from acting on this decision for a few months, but over that period he confided it gradually to most of the people he knew, and in this way it took on the galvanising force of a fact with an existence independent of himself.

The offer of an introduction to the editor of an English paper in Rome gave a more precise focus to his thoughts. Addresses, further contacts, and helpful tips followed on, some of them from quite unexpected quarters; the woman he did his market research for had once lived in Rome herself and gave Jonathan the address of a rental agency that specialised in flats in the old quarter, the Centro Storico. Someone else knew of a language school in Parioli that paid a living wage . . .

A plan for living in Rome began to develop, unfolding with a surprising ease and rapidity, which gave it in Jonathan's mind a seal of rightness and predestination.

He enrolled in a short course for teaching English as a

foreign language. As part of it he was filmed giving a class to his fellow students. Once again he saw himself as if from the outside, and once again he was dismayed at what he saw: there was something in his bearing that was so shy and innocent, so timidly self-effacing, that he became quite alarmed and felt more than ever the urgent necessity of putting himself through an experience that would toughen and anneal him.

There had been a slight cooling in his relations with Katie after their evening at the auction house, but in the weeks before Jonathan's departure, they began to see each other regularly again. Soon they were meeting more frequently than ever.

Katie would ring him late in the afternoon and ask if he wanted to have a drink or see a film, and even if he had made some other arrangement, he would usually get out of it. The truth was, he still cared more for Katie's company than anyone else's. He found her casual acceptance of all the less reputable instincts of her own psyche strangely soothing and relaxing. Careless, egotistical, amoral, and transparently manipulative as she may have been, he would always feel a definite freeing of certain internal constrictions when he was with her, as if at other times he was permanently anxious and on his guard. He knew that he would prefer to spend an evening with her than with anyone else, even if that meant the risk of being hurt.

Under the pressure of his imminent departure, their friendship took on a new, valedictory sweetness. The latent attraction between them, which had never been quite extinguished, flared up as the days went by.

Jonathan was offered a lease on a flat near the Ponte Sant'Angelo, starting from the beginning of October. Late one afternoon in September he went to meet Katie in her office for a drink.

She greeted him warmly, wearing a girlish frock he hadn't

seen before, ruched at the front like a pinafore, with bright cotton embroidery.

Jonathan sat in one of the low leather chairs while she went to the drinks cabinet. When she came over with the drinks she knelt on the floor beside him.

'So, Jonathan, you really are abandoning us.'

She spoke in a quiet voice, looking at the ground.

'Well . . .' He hadn't seen it in quite those terms, but he felt flattered by the idea, even if he knew Katie well enough to sense also the intention to flatter. 'I'll be back from time to time.'

'Yes, but it won't be the same. You'll just be passing through. You'll find us all unimportant.'

'No, I won't, Katie.'

'Yes, you will. Then after a while you'll just forget about us.' This was stated as a simple fact.

'I think it's more likely you'll forget about me.'

'Very funny.' Katie looked up, and to Jonathan's surprise she seemed hurt by his remark.

'Katie, I'm sorry—' He touched her shoulder and smiled at her.

They went to a pub and sat at a table out in the garden. It was a warm evening. The tops of buses were visible over the trellised palings of the garden. When the breeze blew, an occasional prematurely brown leaf would fall from the plane trees outside and lie on the ground like a dropped glove.

They drank and talked steadily.

'What are you going to *do* in Rome, Jonathan?'

'Teach; write articles, I hope.'

'No, but what will you do with yourself? You'll get a lovely Italian girlfriend, won't you? A student with a bicycle and long black hair, and every night you'll go to the Tre Scalini and eat tartufi with whipped cream.'

'I don't even know what a tartufo is.'

'You'll find out.'

She put her hand over his. 'Jonathan, I can't bear to think of you going.'

He turned his hand over to hold hers, which was cool, with long, straight, well-manicured fingers.

'I'll certainly miss you,' he said.

'I'll miss you too.'

They slid their fingers together, looking at each other.

After closing time they walked towards Baker Street. They didn't speak. The air was warm, and the quiet streets still smelled of summer foliage. Streetlamps were couched deep in the branches of trees along the pavements, their light crevicing the dark domes into planes of shoaled leaves, silhouetting them, turning their thin fringes amber. At Baker Street Katie hailed a taxi. They stood by the open door and started to say goodbye. Katie brought her lips to his. The smell of her perfume went sharply through him. She put her hands on his shoulders, turning her head slowly beneath his, and he felt the soft body of her tongue against his own. The taxi waited by them on the kerb with its engine running and its meter turning. A feeling of melting sweetness came into Jonathan. The moment seemed both inevitable and utterly surprising. 'You could come with me,' Katie said. They climbed into the taxi together, and the city's lights slid across the tinted windows.

Katie lived in a basement flat near the Old Brompton Road, with an entrance down a sunken stairwell. Jonathan hadn't been here before. There was a little parquet-floored hall that smelled of polish. One side of it was taken up by a portrait of a scarlet-jacketed cavalry officer on a rearing horse.

They went into the living-room and lay on a sofa in near-darkness. They kissed seriously and intently, Katie entering into this role with her characteristic ease of transition. A concentrated attentiveness took possession of Jonathan. The situation seemed to be surging just ahead of him, drawing him along in its wake. He slid the straps of Katie's frock over her shoulders and even at this moment was a little surprised at the action of his own hands.

They made love quietly, almost stealthily, with suppressed cries, as if a part of the pleasure lay in a certain pretence of furtive concealment. Afterwards they bathed together in a deep, old-fashioned bath on four claws, with a curved lip and tall taps that made Jonathan think of two butlers. Water gushed from them and the pipes knocked. Katie lay on her back in his arms, humming to herself while he ran soap over her shoulders and breasts. In a way he felt more intimate with her bathing than making love; more that had been withheld seemed now laid bare.

For several minutes they lay in silence. Vague sensations floated through Jonathan's mind. The sight of Katie's green toothbrush, standing in a glass by the steam-shrouded mirror over the basin, drifted into him on a ripple of inexplicable tenderness. He felt numbed, and richly content.

'What if you didn't go?' he heard Katie say lazily. 'What if you didn't go to Rome?'

He smiled and kissed her wet earlobe. Her nails played lightly across his thighs.

The water cooled. They got out and rubbed themselves dry. Katie put on Jonathan's shirt and went to the kitchen, showing Jonathan to the bedroom and saying to wait there for her.

This was an untidy room, unaired, with a smell of sleep and stale scent. Clothes and magazines were strewn about. There was a marble bust hung with necklaces and an old green cabin trunk marked *Mombasa*, with scarves and sleeves dangling from under the lid like tentacles from a sunken sea-chest.

Up above the bed hung the chandelier, its candle-bulbs blazing and the sharp little knots of gilded ironwork shining brightly. For a moment it was like seeing an old enemy, and a reflexive annoyance flared in Jonathan briefly. But on consideration, its bracketing of the elapsed time since he had last seen it gave a sense of progress that was actually quite satisfying. Here he was, after all. The thought filled him with an almost proprietorial pleasure. He stretched out on the candlewick bedcover, fully naked, warm and languid from the bath.

The palms of his hands were softened and still acutely sensitised, tingling with the memory of the flesh they had held and caressed. In them and in the tips of his fingers his sense of Katie, and of what had occurred, seemed stronger than in his mind. They seemed to hold the impress of the whole evening like that of a physical object. He remembered carrying the heavy chandelier from the auction house. The thought came to him that he lived almost entirely by physical sensations. Even his emotions were really no more than codified clusters of physical sensations. Warmth and cold; hunger and repleteness; pain and pleasure. He wondered if this was true of people in general, or if he was in some way more rudimentary and animal-like in his consciousness than others. He did seem animal-like to himself. He was like a private and solitary animal: something dark and velvety, nocturnal perhaps, neither hostile nor friendly; a little fastidious . . .

Katie reappeared with French bread and a pan full of scrambled eggs. She lay by him and they tore off bits of bread to scoop up the eggs, which were hot and buttery, with chopped chives and freshly ground pepper mixed into them. They tasted good, and Jonathan ate eagerly.

'We're starving,' Katie said.

Lying there beside her, Jonathan formed the impression that their being together like this—himself naked, Katie wearing his shirt—had a denser reality than most of the scenes he had lived out so far in his life. Whereas those had all been more or less improvised out of the chance furnishings of the moment, this had come, it seemed to him in his slightly exalted condition, as the result of ancient preparations and stately, inflexible natural laws, like a solar eclipse or the appearance of a comet.

As far as he had analysed things before, he had thought that his attraction to Katie was more or less confined to the erotic sphere, with both the force and the limitation that that implied. Now he wondered if there was something more to it. Not love—the blossom said by someone to break miraculously from the sturdy timber of mutual regard—there was none of that upward-aspiring freshness or candour. But he felt something over and above the physical revelry of gratified desire. Thinking about it now, he saw that it was like a fascination, but a fascination that travelled inward rather than outward, that promised to lead back into himself; an inverted narcissism perhaps, with a sweet blemished taste in it like the fruits that can be eaten only in a state of decay, or like an ember's fascination with air. It answered a need that he suspected now had been present in him long before he had met Katie, though he had not been aware of it until then.

She put the pan on the floor and turned to him. One hand supported her chin while the other started stroking his hair.

'Don't go to Rome,' she said.

He smiled as he had before, looking upward at the ceiling.

'Don't go, Jonathan. Stay here in London.'

She spoke in a quiet voice, turning a lock of his hair about her finger.

'Stay here in London, Jonathan, why don't you?'

He turned to her and saw that although she was smiling she was not joking.

'Katie,' he said. He took her head in his hands and looked at her.

'You don't have to go away, Jonathan.'

He was touched and surprised. He didn't know what to say.
He put his arms around her and they kissed again, more slowly
than before, as if they had found something new to kiss about.
She drew away, gripping his arms.

'Don't go.'

'Katie, what do you mean? Are you being serious?'

'There's no need for you to go, you could just stay here.'

She looked at him with an expression of doting fondness.
He kissed her throat. She lay back, sinking into the pillow.
He undid the buttons of the shirt and saw her naked again,
as if for the first time. He was struck by how lovely she was;
how simple and at the same time extraordinary it was to be
seeing her breasts rising from two ridges in her rib cage, the
nipples dark and oval like whorled knots in pine. He took them
in his mouth, one and then the other.

'Ah God.' She clutched him, her fingernails sharp in the
small of his back.

'Say you won't go, Jonathan.'

Her eyes were closed; screwed tight, as if she were willing
his acquiescence with all her strength. A part of him remained
quite cold and detached and disbelieving. Into another part,
however, which stood in relation to this first like an alembic
beginning to seethe mysteriously under the eye of a sceptical
but intent observer, came the first stirrings of a strange con-
fusion. What he felt now began to commandeer the excitement
and adventurousness he had been experiencing for his imminent departure for Rome, while that departure in turn
seemed to be taking on the sadness and staleness he had once
felt for the idea of staying in London.

'Say it, Jonathan. Say you'll stay.'

She moved from under him, kissing his chest and stomach.
She took him into her mouth. Everything around him, all the
clutter of the room—magazines and clothes, the marble bust
and green cabin trunk, the gold chandelier glittering like a

knived chariot wheel—seemed vibrant and aflame. She drew back again, panting, her cheeks flushed, her eyes dark and blazing.

'Jonathan, I don't like anyone except you.'

He looked at her and felt the softness of his nature yielding beneath hers. Is this what I am? he thought. He wondered what had happened to him and when it had happened.

'Say it, Jonathan, say it. Say you'll stay.'

He opened his mouth to speak, not knowing what he was going to say until he heard himself saying it.

Two days later he phoned and arranged to meet her for lunch in a wine bar. She turned up late, wearing high heels and a business suit. Glancing at her watch, she remarked how she envied him setting off for a new life in a new country.

He looked at her, not quite believing he had heard correctly. She met his eye with an expression of calm indifference. After she had drunk half a glass of wine, she excused herself, saying that she had to interview someone in St Albans.

At home he took the shirt that still smelled of her from under his pillow and threw it in the laundry basket. He looked in the mirror and told himself that what he saw was the face of a fool who had been given an undeserved reprieve for his folly. Half believing it, he sat at his desk and drew up a final list of things that needed doing before he left for Rome.

The expatriate life suited Jonathan. After a few months of settling in, he began to feel as if he was emerging from a long hibernation. He was calm and happy. For the first time in years he felt free of a pervasive melancholy that had coloured even his more contented moments in the past.

He got a job at the language school in Parioli. The work was uninteresting but it paid his expenses, and the impersonal atmosphere of the place was made up for by the camaraderie of the offices of the English weekly newspaper off the Corso Vittorio Emanuele. Here, after he had written some short pieces that the editor had liked, he was given part of the 'Visitors' section to produce, and then a section of his own.

At the Food and Agricultural Organisation, where his editor had sent him for a series on international agencies based in Rome, he met Lydia, a Canadian agronomist. She was younger than Jonathan, fair-haired, with mild blue eyes and a high, smooth forehead. She owned several white dresses and wore a straw hat in the Roman sunshine.

A lofty tone was set during their courtship. Lydia's assumption about love was that it was above all a matter of growth and mutual improvement. Earnest discussion and vigorous, forthright debate were her preferred means. A good argument about aid policy or the military/industrial complex brought more pleasure into her cheeks than wine or flowers. 'Say something contentious,' she would sometimes command Jonathan, who seldom initiated such discussions. She gave him a list of her favourite books and asked him for a list of his, ordering them at once from the Lion bookshop on the Via del Babuino and reading them as they arrived.

'I love you, darling,' she would say as they lay in each other's arms between the clean sheets of her bed. Jonathan would pass his fingers over her clear forehead and through her long, brushed hair.

'I love you too,' he would say.

But even at their most intimate there remained something formal about the way they behaved with each other. At times she seemed to him glazed in a radiance of virtue and wholesomeness that was simply impenetrable, and it would feel oddly futile to make love to her. A little like taking part in some kind of civic ceremony, he thought.

Sensing this perhaps, she made a surprising suggestion one afternoon.

'Darling, why don't we go to bed and get drunk. Wouldn't that be fun?'

With a determined look she emptied several glasses of Scotch into her stomach. She became rapidly drunk, and this unleashed, briefly, an uncharacteristic lasciviousness in her.

Afterwards she was badly sick, and for several days she could hardly bring herself to speak to Jonathan, as though the experiment had been his idea and not hers. He didn't protest; under the apparent unfairness of her tacit accusation, he sensed a true and just apportioning of blame.

Some time after this, in a bar in Trastevere, he saw a girl with a pretty, freckled face and bare arms with thin silver bracelets on the wrists. She was by herself, and from time to time she glanced in his direction. He went over to her table and asked if he could join her. He had never done such a thing in his life. The girl made a pleasant, rustling gesture of acceptance. She was wearing a strong perfume, and he sat down by her with a sense of subsiding into a sweet, fragrant cloud. She was Dutch, a student on holiday. As they talked, Jonathan felt as if he was converging into some hitherto purely hypothetical version of himself, and flooding it with reality.

He didn't contact Katie on his visits to London. They had almost no mutual friends, and he heard little news of her. For a couple of years an occasional scrap of gossip reached him via the cousin who had first introduced them. But the cousin gradually lost touch with Katie, and then Jonathan lost touch with his cousin.

Four years passed. When he thought of their night together or their evening at the auction house in Fulham, Jonathan no longer felt any resentment at Katie's behaviour or chagrin at his own. He would go over his memory of the events quite dispassionately, with a scientific curiosity. It would seem to him that certain facts about his nature at that time had been brought to light, and regardless of how unflattering those facts might be, it was satisfying to know them.

Owing to a crisis in the Italian timber industry, the government was offering tax subsidies to publishers provided they bought Italian wood pulp. The proprietor of the English paper took advantage of this to launch a colour magazine. For the first issue the editor decided to run a piece on Italian and English Palladian houses, along with the people who lived in them. Jonathan put himself forward for the English part of the assignment, as it would pay for a visit to his parents, whom he had not seen for almost a year. The editor gave him the job.

He arranged his interviews and flew to London. For several days he drove around England in a rented car. It was October, mild, with a drizzling mist that followed him south from Derbyshire.

The owners he visited received him warmly, pressing him to stay for meals and sometimes for the night. They were eager to show him their painstaking repairs to cracked cupolas and pilasters worn down by acid rain. He was guided through libraries smelling of beeswax and drawing-rooms furnished assiduously in period style, even when that had meant a sacrifice of comfort. Palladian window entablatures were pointed out to him; he was given tours of grounds with porphyry fountains, ornamental lakes, and sheep huddling in drenched grass under cedars and limes. One elderly couple spent the whole afternoon of his visit talking very slowly about their grandchildren, and then, when it was pitch dark outside, insisted on showing him their garden by the light of a tiny electric torch. He took his own pictures, except when he wanted landscape shots, when he would return with a professional photographer.

The journey led him mostly along minor roads that wound through open countryside and small towns. It was pleasant and strange. He was struck by the thought that he no longer lived in this country. The damp air with its pervasive smell of burning leaves brought the sombre fields and hedgerows sharply into his senses. Now and then a sight would fill him with a nostalgia that was sometimes mixed with an unaccountable anxiety: a yellow and brown copse with a black pond glinting between the tree-trunks, a soft-drinks bottling plant in a cropped field full of Chinese geese . . .

He wondered what the undetectable something was that makes a place a place . . . You come to a group of dwellings, hardly a village—silent, a pale rain-shine on the brick walls. There is a stock car with a joke shark's fin on the roof. A CRYSTAL REFRIGERATION truck dwarfs its owner's bungalow. The place is quiet, deserted, but undeniably a *place*, with a little atmosphere and language of its own that is spoken by the stock car and the refrigeration truck, and then, in another voice, by glistening green dollops of pruned yew trees that seem to contain, swelling through their feathery branches, some liquid light essence of rain and greenness. And then, as you turn a corner, the place with its miniature but self-sufficient economy of shapes and surfaces has vanished, leaving you with a feeling of pleasure, or loss, or even dread, as if something in it corresponded to something in yourself . . .

On a Sunday afternoon, towards the end of his journey, he drove through the Chilterns into Berkshire and came to the gates of a house called Felstead, a few miles outside Wantage.

A drive wound through ploughed fields and past a farm with two grain silos gleaming like pewter in the whitish afternoon light. The drive climbed through a belt of beech trees, smooth-limbed, with black, squid-like eyes where lower branches had fallen or been lopped. Rolling parkland followed, leading to the house itself, which was built of sandstone and gave off a soft yellow glow through the mist. It was smaller than the size of the estate had led Jonathan to expect, though it was in better shape than some he had seen. The tall, panelled windows in the symmetrical wings gleamed with clean glass and fresh white paint. Rawer-looking blocks among the masonry of the semi-circular front portico suggested recent renovation.

Jonathan parked his car and went up the three steps to the domed entrance. A man came to the door, smiling and extending a hand.

'Mr Bennett?'

Jonathan nodded and said yes.

'Francis Trenillin. How do you do?'

The owner of the house shook Jonathan's hand firmly. He was a tall man, quite portly in the middle, tapering to dainty feet at one end, and at the other a narrow, long head with sparse hair that might have once been red. A moss-coloured tweed jacket hung, a little shabbily, from his slightly stooped shoulders, and at first Jonathan took him for a much older man than on closer inspection he turned out to be.

'I thought perhaps we'd see the park first, then go over the house when we come back for tea. You'll stay for some tea, I trust?'

'That would be nice.'

They set off along an avenue of chestnut trees. The grass was covered with fallen chestnuts, and Mr Trenillin collected several of these, discarding the prickly pods and putting the glossy nuts into the pockets of his jacket.

'I thought perhaps we'd have them roasted for tea . . .'

The avenue led to a lake with a small island connected by a balustraded bridge. Some orange-billed moorhens swam for the rushes on the far banks as the two men approached. On the island was a weeping willow—all spokes now—with a wrought-iron seat beneath it. Mr Trenillin came to a halt and stared out across the water. Red and yellow leaves floated on the lacquer-black surface. Splintery reeds and brown bull-rushes with their match-like tops beginning to disintegrate grew thickly along the shore. Mr Trenillin stood in silence, looking across the lake. Jonathan waited beside him. The silence continued for several seconds. Jonathan waited respectfully. From a certain solemnity in the man's presence, he sensed a good-natured and possibly gloomy personality.

'Do you know these plants?' Mr Trenillin said after a while, pointing to the ground. 'They grow in sections which you can pull apart as if they were assembled rather than grew like that. Look . . .' He stooped and showed Jonathan how the thin, fringed tubes of the strange-looking plant slotted together.

'I believe they're called mare's tails.'

They walked around to the other side of the lake and up a steep hill that gradually opened a view onto the whole property.

As they climbed, Jonathan questioned his host about the house and land, and his life there.

Mr Trenillin's grandfather had bought it after returning from East Africa with money from copper and manganese mining. His son, Mr Trenillin's father, had sold the mining business and put the money into property in London, most of which now belonged to Mr Trenillin himself. There was an office in Wigmore Street to which Mr Trenillin commuted three or four days a week. A frown crossed his face as he spoke of it, and it was apparent that he didn't enjoy his duties as a landlord.

'My wife likes London and we keep a *pied-à-terre* there, but personally I much prefer it here. This is where I was born, and I have to say I'm rather childishly attached to it.' He cast a sidelong look at Jonathan, who realised he was being appealed to for reassurance.

'That seems perfectly natural to me.'

'I've been researching into the history of the place. It's quite interesting—'

A happier look came over Mr Trenillin as he talked about his researches and his plan for restoring the park and building to their original glory.

'Grandpa was a complete vandal. If he didn't like a room the way it was, he simply bashed a wall down or punched in a new window. We don't have the original drawings so we're having to consult historians and ferret out descriptions by visitors in the eighteenth and nineteenth centuries. I'm not a scholar, but I have to say I'm enjoying myself tremendously. My sister helps me. She's been staying here with us—and she's better on the house than I am. My speciality is the park, and the question here is which original do you restore it to: Repton? Bridgeman? Capability Brown? They all worked here, or at least their followers did, each of them digging up and pulling down their predecessor's work—'

He became quite animated now as he pointed out plantings

155

of trees characteristic of this or that period, showed where a wall had been replaced by a ha-ha to open the view from the house to the surrounding countryside, speculated on whether a rise here might be the remains of a mediaeval saltory, whether the chestnut avenue might once have formed part of a *patte-d'oie* of avenues fanning out from the house . . .

They reached the top of the hill. A strong breeze blew, whipping drops of rain into their faces. Mr Trenillin was out of breath and stood panting, his cheeks glowing brightly.

'Up here there was a folly once. Look, you can see where the foundations must have been . . .' He gestured toward a circular dip in the earth. 'Somebody must have pulled it down. I can't think why. I should think it was a little Greek temple. Possibly something more pagoda-like, but with a folly I think it's permissible to go with your own preferences and I prefer the idea of a temple. Anyway, we've decided'—here a look of excitement came into the large man's eyes, as if he were letting Jonathan in on a secret—'to commission a miniature replica of Bramante's Tempietto. That ought to interest them in Rome.'

Jonathan made a polite murmur. Between the man's bulky stature, which seemed to suggest quite a jovial soul, and the rather finicky connoisseurship to which he appeared to have dedicated himself, there was an incongruousness that suggested to Jonathan an element of strain.

Lights had come on in the panelled windows of the house. The greens and browns of the surrounding countryside were easing into a grey sleep. Rain had begun to fall steadily.

In the distance, beyond the lake, a pair of headlights appeared from around a hill. Their brightness in the bluish dusk obscured the car itself, which travelled about a quarter of a mile towards the house before veering off in another direction. Mr Trenillin, who had been following the car's progress, turned away without a word and led Jonathan back down to the house.

They went through the portico into a chequered marble hallway. A woman appeared from a corridor.

'Ah, there you are,' she said in a mild voice.

She turned with a smile to Jonathan, and Mr Trenillin introduced her as his sister, Cressida. She looked older than him, with short grey hair and the same oval build. A pair of glasses hung on a beaded chain from her neck.

'I wasn't sure whether to put the kettle on. Shall I put it on now?'

'Yes, why don't you? I'll show Mr Bennett around the house.'

As Cressida went off towards the kitchen, her brother called after her, 'Any telephone calls?'

She turned around, putting on her glasses as if she needed them in order to think.

'No, not while you were out,' she said, then took off her glasses and went towards the kitchen.

Upstairs, in a small room that had been turned into a study with a desk, a sofa, and bookshelves around all the walls, Jonathan saw Katie Vairish's chandelier.

Either it was hers or it was another one identical to hers. There were the sharp sprigs of oak leaf and acorns that had dug into him while he had carried it out of the auction house, and there were the little candle bulbs that had burned above Katie's bed the night they had lain there together four years ago.

A tingling went down his spine. He felt the rush of a half-forgotten complex of sensations: the animal sweetness, the feeling of being concentrated or compacted into a narrower part of himself, the peculiar tension. He opened his mouth to ask where the chandelier came from, but stopped himself.

'This is a pleasant room' was all he said.

'My wife's study.'

Jonathan looked at the chandelier again. There was no mistaking it. A dizzying feeling went through him, as if the years since he had last seen it were an interval of distance rather than time and he was looking at it from a vertiginous height.

'She works here, then, your wife?'

'Occasionally. You might meet her later on. She's sometimes home in time for tea.'

They went out of the room and continued the tour of the other upstairs rooms. It was difficult for Jonathan to pay attention. The sight of the chandelier had had the momentarily eclipsing effect of a too-bright light.

They went back down again; down the fanning marble staircase with its round-edged steps like thick ripples of cream, into a drawing-room with stucco wreaths of camellias and mignonettes. Straight-backed sofas and chairs stood on an Oriental rug. In the corner was a spinet inlaid with brown-and-white marquetry. A fire had been lit and the flames gleamed on the dustless surfaces of porcelain vases and walnut cabinets. Looking at these things, thinking of the grounds with the lake and avenue, the rolling acres of grass, the sense of a sublime and fantastical misappropriation arose in Jonathan. He wondered if it was really as he imagined. He tried to picture Mr Trenillin as Katie Vairish's suitor, her husband. Sensing the imbalance, or an equilibrium precariously maintained by money, a feeling of sympathy, even solidarity came into him. At the same time, the impression of some jubilantly contemptuous appetite glimmering behind every detail of the property filled him with a harsh joy.

'This is lovely,' he heard himself say dutifully.

Cressida brought in a tea-tray and poured tea into translucent china cups. She handed one by its saucer to Jonathan and another to Mr Trenillin. The three of them sat around the fire, balancing the cups and saucers on their knees. Outside, it was dark. A glass clock on the mantelpiece struck the hour with a soft, whirring ring, and Mr Trenillin checked it against his watch. The pockets of his jacket bulged with chestnuts, but he appeared to have forgotten about them and Jonathan didn't think it would be polite to remind him.

They talked about the house. Cressida carried most of the burden of the conversation. She herself lived in Oxford, she explained, where she had a fellowship in history at St Hilda's. This year she had taken a sabbatical and was staying at Felstead to help Francis with the restoration.

'We had the mouldings repaired with real egg stucco. I've never seen so many broken eggs in my life . . .'

Mr Trenillin seemed distracted. Cressida looked at him with an expression that wasn't tender, was even a little cold, but nevertheless conveyed a certain sisterly concern. Every now and then the swishing sound of a car on the wet road beyond the lake could be heard, and the three of them would fall silent for a few seconds until the sound faded away.

Jonathan accepted another cup of tea and tried to interest Mr Trenillin in the other houses he had visited for his article. The man nodded his narrow head and smiled vaguely, showing his crooked yellow teeth. He sighed.

'Sunday evenings . . .' he said. 'There's something terrible about them even at the best of times. I wonder why that is.'

'No doubt our punishment for not observing the day of rest,' Cressida answered pertly, with a smile.

Francis Trenillin continued: 'I can be sitting here having spent days and days in absolute contentment, and suddenly find the most awful feeling of dreariness creeping into me like a sort of freezing liquid, and when I ask myself what on earth's the matter, I realise. Of course! It's Sunday evening.'

He sat back in his armchair and looked into the fire, his long legs sprawling from his broad waist and hips, the tiny teacup forcing a curious mincing appearance into his thick, fleshy hand.

There was a silence.

'I should probably start making my way,' Jonathan said. The talk was growing strained, and he had no further pretext for staying at the house. Little effort was made to detain him, but for a while he didn't stir. He sipped the sour dregs of his tea and debated asking Mr Trenillin if his wife was Katie Vairish, but again thought better of it. It seemed to him some awkwardness would be involved in his declaring he knew her. Then too, there was something that appealed to him about not declaring it: her own sport of gratuitous stealth, but also the obscurely satisfying thought that she might discover from her husband who had visited that afternoon and then wonder if he had known whose house he was in . . .

'It's been a very pleasant afternoon,' he said, setting his tea cup on the floor.

Cressida put on her glasses.

'We shall look forward to reading about ourselves. You'll send us the article, won't you?'

They all stood up.

'I'll fetch your coat,' Mr Trenillin said.

As he was walking towards the door, the hum of a car engine came through the rain, which was now falling heavily outside.

The three of them stood still, following the sound with their ears. It rose, and a swishing was heard on the road beyond the lake. It travelled in a wide arc about the house, ebbing and rising, each time slightly fuller on the return, so that it seemed to be approaching in waves. Lights broke through the beech wood separating the park from the farm, and the swishing turned to a sizzling as the car came up to the house. By then Mr Trenillin had forgotten about Jonathan's coat and was on the bottom step of the lit portico, holding an umbrella. Cressida waited in the portico, while Jonathan hung back behind her, in the drawing-room doorway. Through the hall window he saw the slim, familiar figure climb out of the car into the shelter of the waiting umbrella. He saw her kiss her husband on the lips and slip her arm through his as they walked briskly up the steps to the house. Mr Trenillin was smiling eagerly.

'Oh, you poor thing. You poor thing,' he was saying as Katie gave an amused, voluble account of traffic jams and motorway diversions.

They entered the portico, where Mr Trenillin paused to shake out the umbrella. Katie lightly relinquished his arm and took in its place her sister-in-law's.

'Cress, hello. How are you?'

'I'll put the kettle on for you,' Cressida said, patting Katie's hand and disengaging herself.

'Oh, and I got chestnuts for you,' Mr Trenillin cried, catching up with Katie, who took off her jacket and hung it on the coatrack.

'You sweet thing.'

Passing into the hallway, Katie came to a halt. She stood still, looking across the hall in silence.

'Ah yes,' her husband said, 'you're just in time to meet Mr Bennett. He's the journalist . . . You remember . . . Mr Bennett, my wife, Katie.'

Jonathan stood in the doorway while Katie came towards him. He saw that she had changed a little. The years that had passed seemed to have brought into final balance and definition all the delicate features of her face. Her cheekbones were more prominent than before, and the line of her jaw was a little harder, giving her face a gem-like, ghostly beauty.

He was about to feign the surprised recognition that the moment seemed to call for when Katie said, 'How do you do, Mr Bennett,' holding out her hand with a steady gaze in which the mirth was only visible as a faint suppressed movement about her lips.

'How do you do,' Jonathan heard himself say. He shook her cold hand and followed her, or was somehow swept, back into the drawing-room. He felt as if he were in a dream where something at once dangerous and immensely gratifying was taking place. Mr Trenillin was at the fire, kneeling on the floor and rooting at the embers with a copper shovel. Katie sighed and breathed in the warmth of the room. Her eyes shone, full of the dark night that she had been driving through, lit at the back with a subdued but teeming glimmer that Jonathan remembered well, and that seemed to beckon on to some bright perpetual revelry within. She ran a finger along the keys of the spinet, then touched an arrangement of Helleborus roses in a vase and turned to Jonathan.

'So my husband has been showing you the place?'

He nodded.

'And you're writing it up for a paper in Rome?'

'That's right. An English paper.'

'I see. That explains why you're English. I was expecting an Italian.'

He didn't know what he should say or do. Apart from her evident amusement at pretending he was a stranger, it was hard to tell what she was feeling. Perhaps nothing more than that amusement. The watchful dependency on her whims and moods that had consumed him when they were together in the past rose in him on a strong, sweet current of memory. He saw that her self-possession had reached a point of apotheosis where it was indistinguishable from cruelty.

'Won't you stay for supper?' she asked.

'Well—I was just on my way . . .'

Jonathan looked to Mr Trenillin, and Katie too turned to her husband, her hand resting on one of the cabinets in a lazily proprietorial way.

'You didn't invite the man to stay for supper, darling?'

'Well, I—'

'Shame on you! Sending a fellow out on a night like this without a morsel to eat.'

Her husband had turned his head while his body remained kneeling towards the fire, his large behind facing out into the room. He looked sheepish.

'Dear,' he said, 'I'm sorry. I didn't think . . .'

He took a handful of chestnuts from his jacket pocket and tumbled them onto the tarnished copper shovel.

'Well then. And I've told you before, darling, not to stuff things into your jacket pockets. It ruins them and makes you look ridiculous. Like a schoolboy.'

Mr Trenillin frowned and turned back to the fire. Katie sighed and looked at Jonathan.

'I hope you'll join us, then?'

She held his glance. A brilliant, unashamed hilarity showed in her eyes. Again he felt as if he were in a dream, or else the faint delirium of a sickness, the symptoms of which were distributed as much beyond him as within; taking in the bright room, with Mr Trenillin kneeling on all fours at the centre, Katie poised with her hand on the swirling-grained surface of the cabinet, Cressida approaching with the tea-tray and pausing at the sight of the two apparent strangers staring into each other's eyes, the chandelier upstairs with its gilt sprigs of leaf and acorn, and the cold, rainy night outside; and as he accepted her invitation, looking half at her and half at her sister-in-law, who was standing alert and motionless at the edge of the Oriental carpet, he felt that if it was a sickness in him that these things denoted, then the sickness was entering a new and more definitive phase. And among other things this filled him with a curious, sombre satisfaction.